MONO LAKE

Stories by

Martha Clark Cummings

Rowbarge Press
PO Box 407
Monterey, CA 93942

Published by Rowbarge Press
P.O. Box 407
Monterey, California 93942-0407

First printing June, 1995

Copyright © Martha Clark Cummings, 1995
All rights reserved

The author gratefully acknowledges support from the Astraea Lesbian Writers Fund; Money for Women/Barbara Deming Memorial Fund; The City University of New York Professional Staff Congress; and The New York Foundation for the Arts.

Several of the stories in this book have appeared previously in slightly different form: "The Duchess" in *Out of the Dark: Survivors of Family Violence*; "An Incident" in *Pearl*; "Runaway" in *North Atlantic Review*; "Absence Makes the Heart" in *Kalliope*; "Made to Measure" in *The Connecticut Writer*; "Swimming in Winter" in *Sojourner*.

Library of Congress Card Number: 95-68710
ISBN   0-9646201-2-X

Printed in the United States of America

PUBLISHER'S NOTE
This is a work of fiction. Names, characters, places, and incidents either are the products of the author's imagination or are used fictitiously, and any resemblance to actual persons, living or dead, events, or locales is entirely coincidental.
Without limiting the rights under copyright reserved above, no part of this publication may be reproduced, stored in or introduced into a retrieval system, or transmitted, in any form, or by any means (electronic, mechanical, photocopying, recording, or otherwise), without the prior written permission of both the copyright owner and the above publisher of this book.

For Lisa

MONO LAKE	1
ABSENCE MAKES THE HEART	27
AN INCIDENT	49
LOVE STORIES	71
THE DUCHESS	85
SWIMMING IN WINTER	103
RUNAWAY	123
MADE TO MEASURE	143
LILLIAN'S PIANO	157

MONO LAKE

Here in Lee Vining the best place to have breakfast is Red's. I like to sit at the counter alongside the kitchen door where I can watch the slices of rye, sourdough and white bread work their way around the old fashioned toaster. Every morning the toast takes a ride on a ferris wheel.

Jaye wears a uniform like all the other waitresses. She just looks better in hers. They all wear white blouses and maroon wrap skirts and whatever shoes they want. Jaye wears brown shoes that tie up. Not the most attractive but then she wears her thigh-highs with them and sometimes when she's moving fast I can see a flash of her bare leg. Watching her work makes my day. It feels like nothing else matters.

I tie my hair up and smooth lotion over my skin until it glows. Everybody says I have great skin. Then I go down to Red's for my sourdough toast. I order the same thing every time I go because it makes me so happy to hear Jaye say, "The usual?" The hashbrowns sizzle on the griddle, and I watch her take my toast and brush it with the melted margarine and I promise myself that today will be different. I will turn into someone Jaye could love.

Jaye is mixed-blood, like a lot of us. Multi-racial, as they say on the TV now. When we were in school we used to tease each other. Nobody wanted to be related to the Indian tribe that scoops the brine fly larvae off the lake and makes a mash out of them for food. But we are. Some of us, anyway. Others, like Jaye, seem more black. Others, more Mexican-looking. It doesn't matter. Nobody in this town is completely white and nobody pretends to be. It's no big deal as long as you don't try to live somewhere else where you have to choose your neighborhood and your friends according to what color you are. Maybe that's part of why nobody leaves.

Sometimes I like to think of us all as part of the exotic landscape, like the salt lake and the tufa that draw the tourists to this town. I can practically recite what's in the tourist brochure, I've seen it so often, now that I clean motel rooms for a living. This is about what it says: Salty lake water (carbonates) plus fresh water springs (calcium) make tufa (pronounced toofah) (calcium carbonate). Mono Lake's tufa towers, with their knobs and spires, are spectacular examples of what nature can do with a few basic elements.

So are Jaye and I. Just a couple of human tufa towers. We stand there, tall and strange and beautiful, mysterious shapes formed by a mixture of elements that is ordinary but almost never happens. For a few short months in the summer, the tourists come, holding hands and wearing hiking boots, and stare at us, their mouths gaping. And then the road is closed for the winter and that's that.

One night Jaye told me she would go away with me if I stopped doing junk for a month. I could hardly believe my ears. "You would?" I kept saying. She leaned over and gave me a big kiss on the mouth to prove it. But I haven't been able to stop yet. I haven't even been able to try. Every morning when I go in to Red's

I can tell she's waiting for me to tell her I quit. It's starting to weigh on us. And pretty soon it's going to be winter again and we're all going to be sitting around unemployed, snowed in, and tempted by drugs worse than ever.

Last night, already, there was a cold wind off the mountains, and the temperature was headed down into the thirties. Last year I didn't have to move back into my sister's house until the end of September, but this year I don't know if I can make it that long. My rent-free pine-paneled motel unit is behind the house. It has a hole in the floor so I get to live in it from June until I can't stand the cold anymore. The floor is all crooked, and sometimes when I've had a little too much dope I feel like I'm on a ship that's rolling. If I'm in a good mood I start imagining that Jaye and I are going to answer one of those help-wanted ads that are always in the paper and go work on a cruise ship. I see the two of us in our cute little uniforms serving drinks to the wealthy ladies on a luxury cruise. I see one of them asking me to help her out with something in her cabin, falling for me, and me telling her I'm already taken. I am beautiful. Nobody has ever questioned that.

Mono Lake 5

But there's the drug test thing. I would have to pass the drug test, and the way things are right now I couldn't do that. Melba told me her son, John, went down to Fresno to fill out an application last week, and the first thing they told him was that he had to pass a urine test. So before I do anything I have to get through an evening without getting high. Just once. Just one evening one time without getting out the syringe. Then I could go down by the lake and have a walk without imagining I'm talking to God whenever I see one of the tufas. Dick says nobody ever said the lake was sacred. All the Indians cared about was whether the volcanoes were going to erupt again or not.

Dick is my sister Dee's husband. Except for during the summer, I've been living in the basement of their house ever since I lost my job at the grocery store for skimming a little off the top. Sheryl was sorry to let me go. She understands. She has a habit of her own to support. You can tell by the big blue circles under her eyes and by how skinny she is. She asked me to stay a little later than everyone else one night in March, not last year but the year before already, and then she told me she knew I'd been stealing from her. I tried to tell her I was just borrowing but she wouldn't listen. She just said she wouldn't have Jack, the sheriff, come over and put handcuffs on me, but she was going to have to let me go. We would come up with a reason between the two of us for why I wasn't working there anymore. I don't remember what the reason was, but the next time she gave herself a shot she told everyone about how I'd been borrowing from the cash register, and it doesn't take long for the whole town to find out when the whole town is a hundred and fifty people.

So now the only person who will hire me is my sister, Dee. I clean the rooms in the motel that she and Dick run in the summer. There are eight cabins that sleep four to six people and eight rooms for two. I do them all myself every day of the week from the middle of May to the middle of October, and this year I'll be lining up again with everyone else at the unemployment office unless something changes. Unless I can pull myself together and get myself out of this town and persuade Jaye to come with me. The trouble is I can't tell if she's teasing me or not.

"I thought you were straight," I said that time after she kissed me and she said, "I was 'till I laid eyes on you, sugar," and kissed me again. But what if she doesn't really mean it?

In the meantime I make a living cleaning other people's toilets. This is the cheapest place in town—thirty dollars a night for a double—and there's a little kitchenette unit in each room, a party sized refrigerator with a gas range on top, and the "guests" pile into these rooms and live like pigs. These Europeans, especially. We are listed in some guidebook for European students who want to live as if they were dirt poor. Every time I see these groups of young Germans and Swedes arrive, I cringe.

Seventy percent of the people who come through here are foreign. They come up through Death Valley after seeing "the big hole"—as Mrs. Byrne calls it when she can't remember it's called the Grand Canyon—go by Mammoth, come through here and go on to Tahoe and Vegas. This is the low spot on the grand tour. Most of them don't even speak English. I try to be tolerant, but it's hard to keep answering the same questions over and over again. Sometimes Dee talks me into working the front desk after I finish cleaning all the rooms. And even if I hang a no-vacancy sign on the door and on the window, hoards of them still come in, asking if I don't have a room. In their guidebook it must say if the motel says no vacancy, don't pay any attention. Just play dumb and keep asking over and over if there's a room available. Barge in and start waving your money around.

As I'm scrubbing the sink in Cabin Ten I can hear old lady Byrne talking to some tourists about how cold it was last night. She's lived here for thirty years and hasn't lost one bit of her Australian accent. She runs the Blue Sky Motel, our competition. Except that there isn't any competition in this town. Either every single room in the place is booked, or we're all closed for the season and huddled around our wood stoves trying to get warm. Mrs. Byrne is talking about the weather. It turns out that the low temperature was thirty-seven degrees last night. August fifteenth is a little early for frost, but she's pretending like it's very unusual and that's why none of the rooms have extra blankets. "It's usually very nice," she's telling this German couple, who may or may not know what she's talking about. "Even in winter with all the snow around you can come out in the afternoon in your shirtsleeves." She cackles, her dowager's hump quivering. The couple shivers and smiles appreciatively.

Sometimes even in winter I drive out to the lake, if my sister will let me drive the jeep and the chains are on. I park at Navy Beach, keep the car running and the heat on even when I get out. First I give myself a little pop under the skin. Then I don't care if it's thirty below. I walk down the path and try to see the sand tufa buried in the snow. I know they're under there somewhere, five feet tall and looking like cement organ pipes or the inside of a tooth or like something you find in caves. I flail my arms through the snowdrifts, shouting things like, "I know you're in there! Come out!" and "Take me back! I love you!" and other things that don't make sense.

Everybody says the same thing about this town. In the summer it's a gold mine. In the winter it's a ghost town. Snowdrifts pile up and cover your windows. Trucks go through on the highway, the drivers stopping at the one restaurant and one motel that stay open. And other than the sound of the tire chains flapping on everybody's four wheel drive vehicles, there is the sound of snowflakes falling, which you can actually hear.

On winter evenings I sit downstairs in the "finished" basement of my sister's house and listen to the water humming through the pipes, like blood through veins, amplified, and think, "There's Dick having his shower," or "There's Dee turning the water on and off, on and off, as she washes the dishes, so as not to run up the water bill," and I hate them. I hate their footsteps tromping over my head. I hate their boots on the creaky floorboards, the sound of the dogs' toenails.

When they are quiet, I sneak up the stairs and into their kitchen. I don't have to sneak. Dee says I can come up any time, but the sneaking makes it better for me. I need to take something back from them.

I always wish the summer would last forever but especially this year. It's because of what happened last year right after I moved back to the house, before it started snowing and we closed the motel. Now the house seems evil.

What happened was that I caught them. I didn't mean to. It wasn't like I was trying to get in on the fun. Nothing like that. I woke up and couldn't see anything at all and had one of those panics like you get sometimes. I thought I had gone blind. I looked out into the darkness and could see absolutely nothing. I actually said to myself, "Oh my God, I've gone blind." I reached for the light and turned it on, my heart pounding, and it was like being hit between the eyes with a baseball bat, and then I just sat there feeling very stupid and relieved, but my heart was still fluttering around in my chest like crazy, like they say canaries do just before an earthquake comes. I thought if I could just give myself a little fix, just a half a fix, I would be fine. When this idea catches you at three twenty-three in the morning it seems like an especially good one, so before you know it I was tying the belt around my arm, patting my vein like a kindly nurse, sticking the needle in, filling up again with that cool-hot quicksilver pleasure.

Then I wanted my ice cubes. I like to chew ice cubes and I don't have a freezer. I like to fill up the green bowl, feel them melt one by one between my fingers, pop them in my mouth and suck on them, chew them up. The crunching is a tremendous relief. The echo of the crunching in my head drowns out almost everything. But I could hear the floor creaking that night so I knew they were still up. I told myself to forget about it, not to go up there, they would see that I had just fixed myself and give me hell for it because I keep telling them that I've quit.

But the power surge side of the drug told me different. When a thousand volts of electricity are surging through your brain you think you can do anything. You can conceal anything. Plus, the last thing you should do when you're high is tell yourself you can't have something. Right away it becomes an obsession.

Anyway it was just a baby fix. So I started up the back stairs on my toes. They keep the door unlocked from their side. I installed a deadbolt on mine. I figured I'd just go into the kitchen, get some ice, head back down the stairs, no one would see anything. But they were right there, at the kitchen table. My first thought was that this other girl, the one I'd never seen before, a new friend of Dee's I thought, had lost her contact lens on the kitchen floor, and she and Dee were crawling around looking for it. Why else would they both be on their knees? My first impulse was to offer to help. The kitchen linoleum looks like green marble and its swirls were very appealing to me at that moment. But when I took a step forward I saw Dick. He was sprawled in his chair, his head lolling back like a doll's head, his legs spread wide, the thick coarse fabric of his jeans pulling tight across his thighs, his hands dangling loose, filling up with blood like water balloons, his lips loose and wet, his breathing thick. And the part I don't even want to mention. His zipper pulled down, the thick cotton of his underwear bunched up inside, his swollen erection.

He had socks on like mine. Thick gray wool. They're called thirty-below socks. Everybody in town wears them. I looked and looked at his socks, trying to concentrate on that. But like I said, when you're fixed, your mind has a mind of its own.

They were so busy they hadn't even heard me come up the stairs. I was quiet. I had on my thick wool socks. I had slid back the deadbolt almost silently. Anyway, Dick was the only one facing me and his eyes were closed.

My sister moved forward on her knees, holding the girl by the hand. The girl was younger. More my age. She looked like she had been crying. This happened very fast. It wasn't like I was standing there for hours. The incident just got frozen in my mind, and now it seems like I was watching them forever. My sister leaned over and took his cock in her mouth, sucked it, moved up and down on it like a pro.

"Now you try it," Dee said to the girl. "I showed you how. You do it now."

She was whispering to the girl in a sweet voice, as if she were the girl's mother teaching her to put on lipstick. But she took the girl by the back of the head, grabbed a handful of her hair, and shoved her in the direction of Dick's glistening cock.

What were they giving her in return, I wondered, a free night in the motel?

"Take a deep breath," Dee said in the voice of a swim instructor. "Take a deep breath. It goes in much easier. There you go. There you are," she said.

This was when I started making wild promises to God. "Just let me get away from this," I was whispering in my head. "Just let me go back downstairs without their noticing me. I'll never shoot up again. I swear it. I'll never lay a finger on another drug."

It seemed like a good time to start backing away. I could leave the door ajar. Not even lock it. They would never notice. I could lock it later after they went to bed.

"Just let me out of here," I prayed because I knew they would never forgive me if they knew I had seen them, that I would have no job and nowhere to live, and this was the last place in town that would have me.

But then Dick wanted to sneak a peek. Dick wanted to have a look at this stranger, this girl Dee had lured into the house with what? the promise of an extra blanket? doing him. Down on her knees, guided by his wife's expert fingers, his wife shoving her thumbs all the way to the back of the girl's mouth, his wife working his cock in deeper and deeper, so he opened his eyes, squinting as if they were still shut and he saw her but he also saw me, standing there in the doorway, my mouth drooping open with the droop of a junkie (I know what I look like when I'm high) my eyelids wanting to close even though I was amazed enough to be forcing them open, and he didn't even blink. He didn't stop. He didn't tell Dee I was standing there. He looked me right in the eye and came in the girl's mouth, and she whimpered and shook and tried to pull her head away, but Dee clamped a hand on the back of her head and I went back downstairs, leaned over the toilet bowl and puked my guts out on the girl's behalf.

Dick never said anything. He never told. It's a secret that he and I have now. The two of us know something Dee doesn't. It's almost as good as if he had done it with me. There is nothing I can do about this. If I told Dee what I had seen she would make me move out, and there is nowhere else for me to live. Jaye won't let me live with her until I'm clean. I've asked her.

Dick wants to be the next great Western Photographer. He wants to be a combination of Ansel Adams and Edward Weston. Nudes on the snowcapped Eastern Sierra are his thing. We live in a place where UC classes come to take pictures in the fall before the Tioga Pass closes. Someone with talent could probably be successful here. Dick's pictures always end up looking like pornography though.

He talks a lot about wanting to make strong visual statements, about the correct use of Amidol, about using the zone system. There are people here in Lee Vining who actually believe he's hot shit. All the gift shops carry his less pornographic prints, framed and unframed. Dick talks like a pro and people believe him. He brushes back his hair and talks about black and white materials, exposure judgement, proper metering procedures, use of the gray card. He always calls what he does photographs. They are not pictures or God forbid, snapshots. And like all of us, he can almost make a living off the starry-eyed tourists who come through here for four months every year and it convinces him that he's a great but unappreciated photographer who deserves a break, who deserves not to have to work another job.

I have never posed for him. He has asked me plenty of times, in front of Dee, too. Once he told me he wanted to do a series of me and my motorcycle. This was before I smashed it up. He wanted me nude except for my leather jacket. I burst out laughing.

"Where are we gonna hang it?" I asked him. "On a calendar over at Kelley's Fix-It-Shop?"

He got that look, like a dog that's been beaten.

"You slimy little junkie dyke," he said.

The thing is that Dick and I have one more secret together. One night right after I moved in with them, Dee was at the nearest hospital, twenty-five miles south of us on Route 120 in Mammoth, because her friend Val was having another kid and Dick and I were in the house alone. It was starting to get warm again during the day but once the sun went behind the mountains, forget it. There was still frost and sometimes when we woke up in the morning there was snow on the ground. Dick had been up in Yosemite taking pictures of wildflowers and a woman who, coincidentally, was named Heather. He opened the door cursing the cold. He used to live further south, down near Death Valley. They say people who aren't born here never get used to it. I was on the sofa by the wood stove wrapped in a wool blanket, my feet practically in the fire, so I felt okay. He stamped around in his fancy hiking boots complaining about how his feet were like two lumps of thawing hamburger, and I told him to shut up and get next to the stove. We were joking around. It was when we still sort of got along.

He untied his boots and came over next to me, got under the blanket with me. I trusted him then. He was my sister's husband. I have these ideas about loyalty, anyway. Like when Jaye and I finally get together, I will be true to her forever. I really mean it.

He snuggled up under the blanket, stretched his feet out toward the wood stove.

"Wanna drink?" he asked. I could smell from his breath that he had already had a few. He kept a bottle of whiskey in his truck and a flask in his jacket pocket, like everyone else.

"Sure," I said.

He brought us each a big glass of whiskey. He put a couple of extra logs on the fire. He sat down on the sofa again. I figured we would drink together and have a good talk. We would become better friends. I drank down my whiskey.

Then Dick started in.

"Your face could make me famous," he said. "If I could take the right kind of pictures of your face," he said, chuckling, "we could both get famous."

He went for his camera. I figured if it was just my face he wanted, it would be okay. He looked at me like he was in love with me. This was part of his technique. He took his glasses off to focus the camera. It was the first time I noticed his eyes— beautiful clear blue, iridescent blue like the water in Mono Lake in the springtime.

"You're so beautiful," he said, the shutter clicking. I believed him. I looked into the camera, feeling beautiful. "You're gorgeous. You're as beautiful as the lake. Let me take your picture with the lake. You and the lake. These pictures will change everything."

"When the moon is full," he said, stroking my hair, his hot whiskey breath on my cheek. "When the moon is full. We'll shoot you and the tufa. It will be beautiful."

The place between my thighs was throbbing. He put his hand there. I didn't stop him. He tipped me backwards on the sofa, the camera on the floor beside us, the lens pointing up at us like an eye. He unzipped his pants.

"Reach in and get it," he said. "Stroke it." I did what he told me. He was touching me there. He was doing me with his fingers, through my clothes. I was hot.

"It feels so good," he whispered. "So good."

It's Friday morning, August eighteenth, and I haven't had any junk for twenty-four hours. I don't know how it happened. I don't know where I got the strength. I am sweating and I have the shakes. I dropped a glass in one of the kitchen sinks earlier, shattered it, but I managed to pick up the shards and throw them away without cutting myself. The stink of the rooms seems really bad though. The stink that comes up through the drains, the moldy slimy smell makes me have to run to the commode and puke. They told me to expect this. The people in my group. I went to the meeting at Our Savior of the Mountains. I sat on a folding chair in a damp church basement and I didn't know the ritual yet so I said, "Hi, I'm Annie and I can't stop shooting dope and I'm really really tired of it. Can you people help me or not?" They said they could. They told me the whole thing about one day at a time and they assigned me a sponsor. Melba, the woman who cooks at Yosemite Joe's bar up at the other end of town. I had no idea she was a junkie too. She must have gotten over it a long time ago because she looks great. I mean she's an old broad and everything but she looks healthy. But she has a husband and kids and all. How am I supposed to call her in the middle of the night?

She comes up to me after the meeting.

"Here's what we can do," she says. "Tonight's gonna be the hardest. You're gonna get real cold. You're gonna want someone to scream at. Ed and the kids are camping up near the Sonora Pass. You come stay at my place tonight. We'll have a jacuzzi over at Murphy's."

I burst out crying. This was the nicest anyone's ever been to me. Not even my own mother would be this good. She'd be too freaked by my being a junkie. I stand there sobbing. She hands me a tissue, pats my shoulder, waits.

"You're gonna be all right. You'll see," she said, giving me a big smile, showing the place where she's missing a couple of teeth. "You're gonna be so proud of yourself."

I hold this image in my mind as I hunch over the toilet bowl again, puking my guts out. It's taken me an hour to do two rooms. I've got fourteen to go. I got a late start anyway because of today's meeting.

"It doesn't matter," I tell myself. "It's okay."

I look at myself in the mirror over the bathroom basin of the room I'm cleaning. I run a comb through my hair and slip it back into my back pocket. Tears are running down my cheeks, but not from crying. I splash some cold water on my face, pull on my thick yellow rubber gloves and get back to work.

I wonder if it would be okay to smoke some pot or if I have to be absolutely clean. Melba says they don't even recommend methadone. It's cold turkey or nothing at NA.

In Cabin Six I'm sort of sneaking a peek in the people's luggage to see if they have any drugs. They are a wealthy-looking couple from Palm Springs, staying here only because they got into town late and everything else was already full. Practically every piece of clothing in her suitcase is made of silk or cashmere. Finally I find her cosmetics case. It's bulging with goodies.

I am rifling through all of her pills, sweat dripping from my forehead onto one of her beautiful silk blouses, when I hear a key in the door. I flick the suitcase shut and jump away from it, toward the bed. They may notice, later, that something's been tampered with, but they can't prove anything. I wipe my forehead with my sleeve and stand there trying to look innocent.

It's the husband. Alone. A big guy with a cowboy hat and boots.

"Well, hi there!" he says, looking me up and down like I'm the hooker he ordered.

He's so happy to see me I wonder if he would let me continue looking through his wife's stuff. I just need a little something for my nerves. My vision is getting a little blurry here. I may have lied a little about exactly how much junk I was doing a day. I stand there shaking, my teeth chattering, staring at the man as if he had burst into my living room.

"Don't mind me," he says. "You just go on about your business."

I turn back to the bed and start making it. He goes into the bathroom to take a piss. He leaves the door ajar. Cheap thrills. I keep making the bed like this kind of thing is part of my daily routine. He comes out, zipping up. Then he just stands there, staring at me.

"You sure are pretty," he says. "Your color's a little off, though. Are you sick, young lady? Should you be in bed?" He starts chuckling over this. Like he thinks it's a riot that he said the word *bed*.

"I'm okay," I tell him. "I'm getting over the flu. I'm fine, really."

This is what Melba told me to say. "If anyone asks you what's wrong, you tell them you're getting over the flu. The symptoms are almost identical. Nobody knows anything. Remember that."

"You need to take a rest," he says. His face is purple now. It's clear this guy wants to make a move, but he hasn't the foggiest idea how to go about it. I actually feel a little sorry for him. I could give him some tips. Look, Mister, if you want a girl in this burg it's really simple. Offer her drugs, offer her money, offer her jewelry, take her for a ride to Mammoth in your Mercedes. It's very simple. We're trapped here. Trapped people are easily bought. But for God's sake don't try to charm us. We can't be charmed.

The old guy sits down on the bed, looking defeated.

"Where's your wife?" I ask him.

"She went on a walking tour of the lake. I didn't feel up to it."

"Maybe you're getting the flu," I tell him.

It's like we're old friends or something.

I get busy cleaning the little kitchen area. I have to get the hell out of there and into the next cabin. Dee is going to have a conniption fit when she sees it's time for The Price is Right and I'm only on Cabin Six.

"Young lady?" the old coot is calling me. I imagine he's going to offer me his Mercedes. It has a leather interior. I could just sit in there, sniffing the leather.

"Yes?"

"Could you come in here a moment, please?"

"Be right there."

I stand in the doorway, my yellow rubber gloves dripping on the floor. He is lying on his back on the bed. In one hand he has a hundred dollar bill, in the other, his wife's pearl necklace.

"Five minutes," he whispers hoarsely. "You can have both for just five minutes."

Part of me is still tempted, of course. I could buy myself a pretty nice fix with that bill. Part of me remembers the lesson I heard my sister teaching that girl on her knees. I could do that. "Take a deep breath. Open your mouth really wide." It would be like diving underwater for a few minutes.

But I want to show up at the diner tomorrow morning looking like hell so Jaye will know I finally did it. Because then she's going to give me another big kiss, right in front of everybody in the whole town. I'm sure of it.

"Sorry pal," I tell him. "I'm a dyke. I don't do guys."

I pick up my mop and pail and go on to the next cabin. Chances are my telling him that has made him even hotter. But that's his problem.

Halfway through Cabin Seven I start feeling like I can do anything.

ABSENCE MAKES THE HEART

The captain interrupts the whining rendition of *White Christmas* to tell us that we've been cleared for takeoff. I sit up and tighten my seat belt, pull the collar of my leather jacket up close to my face and put on my sunglasses. Outside, snow swirls across the runway. "Off to sunny Florida," I tell myself with feigned cheerfulness.

There are two girls with perfect hairdos in my row. To distract myself from my fear, I eavesdrop. Ordinarily I would get bored in a minute and stop listening, so the Valium must be working, because I am finding them utterly enthralling. The more I listen, the more I adore them.

As the plane roars down the runway, the prettier, more talkative one in the aisle seat is showing the quiet one next to me photographs of a wedding in which she, a bridesmaid, wore a peach-colored dress. The quiet one agrees it is the best possible way to spend a Saturday afternoon. For a moment I, too, can imagine nothing more glorious. I want to lean over and tell them how happy it's making me that for them, inner life does not consist of thrashing about in the dark muttering, "No, no, this can't be what I was meant to do," as it does for so many of us. I am filled with gratitude that someone, at least, is satisfied. And they are tolerant, too. Here I am, a woman twice their age dressed in a black leather jacket, faded jeans and high-top sneakers, craning her neck so as not to miss a word of their conversation, all of which they accept with great good will. They would probably offer to show me the pictures, too, if I asked.

"What's the difference," the quiet one asks as the plane bumps up through the clouds, "between a spiral perm and a regular perm?"

The one with the photographs shuffles through them like a deck of cards.

We are interrupted by the flight attendant, her cart rattling to a halt beside us.

"Something to drink, sir?" she asks me.

"I'll have a light beer, please," I tell her.

She glares at me as if I had intentionally deceived her, then quickly looks embarrassed, in some version of, "the customer is always right."

"I'm sorry, Ma'am," she says.

"It's okay," I tell her.

The girls with the hairdos give me comforting looks. They knew I was a woman. But I turn away. I don't want to think about them and their photographs anymore. My life seems like a freak show in comparison.

My best friend, Karl, has tried to reassure me by saying that my sister and her husband are much more peculiar than me and Kate. He says that the idea of a big bossy bleached blonde who comes from an exclusive suburb of New York City but acts and talks like she grew up in the Ozarks (this is his description of my sister Dana) and a very short, dark, totally submissive Ecuadorian who may not know how to read, (this is Joey, a/k/a Jose, her husband) going at it in the trailer park they call home, makes people much more uncomfortable than the idea of two average-looking women who love each other. For all I know, Karl is right. But I can't believe that to most people the thought of such a stern straight musician as Kate, playing Beethoven quartets to standing-room-only audiences, a frown on her face and her cello clenched between her knees, and coming home to giggle under the covers with me, is less alarming. Anyway, that's not the point.

    I doze off and don't even bother to open my eyes again until after the wheels have bounced down and we have finished rolling and the whoosh of the engines abruptly stops. People are scrambling to snap open the overhead compartments. The aisle fills up before I have a chance to stand. It doesn't matter since I am in no big hurry to get off the plane. The flight attendant who made the mistake is especially friendly on the way out.

    "Merry Christmas, Ma'am," she says.

    They are waiting for me just far enough from the gate so I have time to imagine they have forgotten to come. This Christmas is my mother's second in Florida, her second without Dad. He never liked celebrating though, so she only started in earnest the year he died, when she moved down here to be closer to my sister,

Dana. They are dressed up because we are going out to dinner, my mother in one of her homemade skirt suits, with color-coordinated shoes and handbag, my sister in an imitation designer outfit with some other animal besides a polo pony on her chest. I can't see Joey. He must be standing behind them. I pull my oversized turquoise sweater way down over my jeans and hope that will be festive enough. Dana sweeps me up, hugs and kisses me, takes my bag out of my hand, behaving like families are supposed to. My mother gives me one of her bleak smiles. Joey raises up on his toes and kisses me on the cheek according to his family tradition. His round soft stomach bumps mine. He has gained some weight since he retired from being a jockey. Then they lead me to the special elevator up to the revolving restaurant where we will get a view of Tampa Bay, then the parking lot, then an empty field, soon to be developed, then the bay again, and so on, depending on how long we stay.

    There are little bunches of red and white flowers on our plates. They are corsages. Part of the arrangement is a tiny package wrapped in gold, the size of one piece of chocolate in a Whitman's Sampler. The little box is empty, though. I'm sorry that Dad is not here. "What, pray tell," he would say, "do small bunches of withering carnations have to do with the birth of our Lord?" Not that he believed in any of that.

I shouldn't think of him right now. Sometimes I can't think about him at all, I can't even look at my own hands, which are large and sturdy and just like his, without my eyes filling with tears.

We order drinks and I put the corsage aside, but I can tell from my mother's carrying on about how pretty it is, and my sister dutifully pinning it to her blouse, that I shouldn't have done that. I look down at it again and see there's a little card that goes with it, and then it hits me. Joey did this. I take a big swallow of my Manhattan, then get out the two long pins with the white pearls on the ends and jab them into my sweater, pinning the thing onto my shoulder. I feel as if Joey, with one gentle push of his small calloused hand, sent me falling back through time, like you do in dreams, to land with a thump on the gleaming hardwood floor of the ballroom at the West Orange Country Club, where my sister and I attended dancing school. I feel my hands begin to sweat inside the white cotton gloves, the crinoline scratching my thighs. I am sixteen years old, looking at myself in the mirror, wearing a yellow satin evening dress with spaghetti straps. I look and look.

Nothing changes. I cannot get over the feeling that I am wearing someone else's clothes.

"Let's talk about Robin's work," my sister says, conscientiously using my full name and not the family nickname, "Rob."

The bookstore where I work part time caters heavily to women. Not wanting to make them uneasy, I tell them that a book by one of our best-selling authors has been made into a movie, and how unusual that is, rather than that we just got a new supply of buttons that say, "We are NOT just good friends!"

"There is so much book of woman?" Joey asks, meaning are there really so many books by and about women to dedicate a whole store to them.

"Joey isn't much of a reader," my sister says generously. Then she starts searching through her bag for her cigarettes and I know they have had enough. Dana, like so many straight women, carries a purse and then spends a lot of time looking for things she has dropped into it, but she also uses it to signal that it's time to change the subject.

During dinner I ask Dana about the driving school where she is an instructor. Once she told me that her students were all teenagers and widows. The teenagers talked about what was going on at school—a dance they wanted to go to, for instance—and the widows talked about the illnesses their husbands died of. Now she says her latest student is a transsexual. I guess this is her way of saying that whatever I am is all right with her, but I kind of resent the analogy.

"Is it a man or a woman in its present form?" I ask her.

"A woman. A pretty one, too."

"Is she a good driver?"

"Yeah. Real good. She drives like a man."

Joey starts laughing, then takes a look at me and stops.

"It's okay," I tell him.

"I'll drive," Dana says, extending her hand for the keys to my mother's Volvo. My mother forks them over. She submits to her eldest daughter's will in much the same way she did to her husband's. I am relieved to be kept apart from the struggle and much too drunk to drive anyway. I sit in the back seat with Joey and try to engage him in a conversation about his leather repair business at the track, although it's hard to think of what questions

Absence Makes the Heart

to ask. He also works as a groom, but I know he doesn't want me to ask about that.

As we go over the causeway Dana takes one hand from the wheel and rummages in her bag for her cigarettes. My mother watches her, engrossed as an infant, then begins digging into her own bag. Now they are both smoking and have forgotten to open the windows.

"Could you crack the windows, please?" I yell from the back seat.

My mother lets out a big sigh and rolls her eyes, but she doesn't make any of her remarks about how healthy I try to be in some ways.

We pull into the carport of what my sister and I refer to as our mother's "immobile home." Practically the minute Dad died, she put the house we grew up in on the market and started shopping for a "doublewide" down here. The house in Ridgefield went for a fortune. She paid for this place by check. It was really hard, she told me, to get all the zeros into the little space they give you.

When we get inside, I realize that what's familiar about my mother's home is that it's made of the same building material the inside of the airplane was. I squeeze the beige plastic windowsill just to be sure. The walls, too, have the same give in them as the walls of the airplane rest room. There is some comfort in figuring out what is so disconcerting about this place. It feels like it's about to take off.

"How do you like our decorations?" my mother asks proudly.

I slouch into a wing chair and look around. The stockings are hung on the artificial wood poles that separate the kitchen from the living room because the little black metal fireplace in the opposite corner, although wood burning and real, is too fragile to support them. The artificial tree is decorated with cone-shaped bubble lights. Joey's favorite, they tell me. My sister flicks them with her finger to get them going.

"Don't always work," she says.

I look at the stockings more closely and notice that my mother has pulled all the threads out of the name, *Rick*, in the stocking she made for my sister's first husband and superimposed *Joey*.

"Great," I tell her. "It looks great."

While she's fixing herself another drink Mom wants to talk to me about sinkholes. It's hard to hear her with the ice tray rattling, but I think she's saying that one side of her house is already lower than the other. Not visibly, of course, but it worries her. Then she tells me about a house that actually folded in half and disappeared into the earth.

"Mother," Dana says. "It didn't disappear. If you walk over to the hole and look down, you can still see the house."

"All right, " my mother says. "But still ..."

Mom is very excited about opening the stockings and keeps claiming that we have this tradition of opening them on Christmas Eve, when we all know that last year we opened them on Christmas morning. My sister and I exchange a quick greedy glance. Dana takes down the stockings and solemnly hands me mine. The first gift I unwrap is a roll of Scotch tape. This, in fact, is a tradition. My sister and I and Joey contrive to open the little packages simultaneously and then howl in chorus, "Just what I always wanted." From Joey it sounds like, "Juice what I wahn." There is an envelope in the toe. My sister and I exchange another look. Even at her most generous, Mom has never given us more than a twenty dollar gift certificate. We pull out the envelopes. Joey has one too. I wonder as we're tearing them open if she would have given one to Kate, had she been here. Probably not. We're not married, after all, so even though we've been living together for years, Kate still doesn't count as family.

I pull out the check and look at it. It is a larger sum than I have ever seen before, more than I earn in the bookstore in a year. All the little zeros in her trembling hand. Mom waits expectantly for our reactions. I look to my older sister for guidance, as I have, I realize now, all my life. She screams. I do, too. She jumps up. So do I. She goes over to Mom and embraces her. That's going a little too far so I hang back and let Joey cover for me. I fold the check carefully and put it in my back pocket, wondering how I will ever be able to persuade anyone again that my mother doesn't love me.

"I finally realized I had enough for all of us," she says bashfully.

My sister wipes the tears from her eyes and says that she and Joey really have to be going. They get up at five-thirty to get him to the track on time, and it's already way past their bedtime. After they're gone, my mother and I just sit there in silence for a few minutes. I don't know what she's thinking about—maybe how it feels to have her own money for once—but I'm remembering one Christmas a few years ago when my father, in a particularly irreverent mood, took my mother and me to the most expensive Japanese restaurant in Manhattan. The green marble tabletops were gleaming, and our sushi was glowing in a spotlight on its little platform. A cluster of black-jacketed waiters hovered at an appropriate distance. My mother reached out to touch the miniature orchids, still not convinced they were real. My father must have had a premonition of his own death, because he suddenly turned to me and said, chuckling, that if I wanted anything I'd better ask him for it now, since he was leaving everything to Mom, and I knew how stingy she was. We all laughed and I said, like I usually did, that there was nothing I needed. It wasn't true, of course. It was just what I said.

I open my mouth to tell my mother what I have just realized—that he was wrong about her—but she gets up to make herself another drink and I lose my momentum.

On Christmas morning, my mother flings my bedroom door open.

"Merry Christmas," she yells.

I open my eyes, pretending she's woken me up but that I'm not mad.

"Merry Christmas," I tell her.

"Coffee?" she says.

"Yeah."

We sit down together in the little dining room. She's telling me how great it is to have a garbage disposal and a dining room table you don't have to worry about making rings on when an old guy dressed as Santa Claus comes by. He's driving a golf cart covered with red felt and strung with tinsel, a boom box playing Christmas carols behind him. He bumps right up onto the lawn and starts yelling, "Merry Christmas" into the kitchen window. My mother gives me one of her most desolate looks, then picks up her camera with trembling hands and totters out the screen door, her quilted bathrobe fluttering behind her. She wants to take my picture with this guy. Last year I would have brooded in the kitchen, but this year I feel like I can afford it. I even let her take my picture with the ceramic pelican in the neighbor's yard that somebody has put a Santa Claus hat on, although I make her wait while I go in to get my sunglasses for that one.

"I should give you big wads of money more often," she says. "It makes you so agreeable."

"It's not about money, Ma," I tell her. But since I can't explain what it is about, she doesn't believe me.

At eleven o'clock Dana strides in, Joey following behind. Then, with all the seriousness of a surgeon, she prepares eggs Benedict. Joey plugs in the Christmas tree lights and turns on the TV. My mother stands beside Dana, trying to be helpful. After breakfast we open the stupid gifts we got each other before we were rich.

On the day after Christmas, my last in Florida, Dana and I drive to the shopping mall in one of the driving school's cars. It's hard for me to keep my hands off the steering wheel in front of me, even though I'm in the passenger seat. The radio is blaring oldies we can sing along to—Roy Orbison, The Four Tops. As we turn into the Countryside Mall, the brake pedal in front of me going down, she tells me she wants an electric blanket with dual controls—"He'll roast us otherwise," she says of Joey. and a coffee-maker that wakes up and gets going by itself. She also wants a camera with a telephoto lens, but she's going to take her time and shop around for that. I remember now that she is always trying to sneak up on herons and egrets and armadillos, always getting her binoculars out to peer at owls' nests.

"You're all right, you know it," I tell her.

She turns off the car and stares at me for a minute.

"All that therapy you've been getting is finally starting to work," she says.

On the way home we stop by to pick up Joey at his repair shop, a twenty-foot house trailer next to the track. When I see him sitting in there among all that heavy machinery, using a small silver hammer on a pair of reins or the buckle of a girth, I can't help thinking of Santa's elves. He has made me a lot of leather gifts. Key chains. Belts. A purse, before he knew I didn't carry one. I remind him of each of these gifts as we're standing there watching him work. He asks if I want him to engrave a metal nameplate, if I'd have anywhere to put it. I can't think of anywhere but I tell him yes.

After picking up Joey we go to Scott's Ice Cream for chocolate malts. Dana is crazy about Scott's ice cream, almost to the point of obsession, she confesses. I decide to order one too, to keep her company. What the hell, I'm thinking. I'm so rich now I can join a fancy health club and aerobicize myself every day, starting tomorrow.

When we get back, Mom comes out the door to greet us, then plops down on the first available wrought iron chair in the little cement area she calls her porch which is really just the end of the driveway with screens around it. She asks me if it doesn't remind me of the screened porch at 206. It doesn't, because the house she's referring to, the one I grew up in, at 206 Hawthorne Avenue, was old, Victorian, and wooden, and the porch was surrounded by trees with broad dark green leaves, so the neighbors couldn't see us when we sat out there in the evening in our pajamas and read. (Dad was around. We still read books.) There, the only disturbance was the moths and beetles banging on the screens, whereas here in Safety Harbor some old person walks by every ten minutes or so and you have to wave and say hello to each one of them. My mother sifts through her mail, tearing open an envelope full of manufacturer's coupons.

"Coupons!" she says. "Who wants coupons?"

She calls them out like an auctioneer. My sister and I pretend to squabble over them, since it seems to give her so much pleasure.

"Bounce!" she calls.

"I'll take it!" I yell.

"I want the Bounce," my sister whines. "I bet you don't even use Bounce."

"Oh, all right," I tell her. "You can have it."

My mother hands it to me.

"You said it first," she says.

When I come out with my bag packed, Mom is watching an old couple go by holding hands. There's a bleak, melancholy look in her eyes, as if a terrible sadness is rising up inside her. Not that she and my father ever held hands. He wasn't even that nice to her. Most of the time he went around saying how disappointed he was that you can't change people. As Henry Higgins he had failed, he said.

I am standing there realizing that my mother could no more go on living in the house in Ridgefield than I could put on my satin dress with spaghetti straps and go be a bridesmaid with the girls on the plane. Dad's scheme, to take a girl from a small town in the depressed Northeast—the very same town he grew up in—and turn her into a lady, did not work out, for him, for her, for any of us.

"I'm sorry, Mom," I tell her, patting her back a little as I say it. She looks up at me with difficulty. Her shoulders are sort of permanently hunched now.

"It's okay," she says. "Kate is a nice girl. I'm getting used to it."

"Thanks," I tell her, still patting. It doesn't even matter that she didn't get what I was talking about.

"Anyway," she goes on. "I'd rather have you living with her than with some bum who can't earn a decent living."

She rolls her eyes toward Joey, who is installing the indoor-outdoor thermometer he just bought her.

"Come on, Ma," I whisper. "He hardly speaks English and he's too old to be a jockey anymore and too short to do anything else. What would you do if you were him?"

"I'd hang around doing favors for my rich mother-in-law."

"But he loves you," I tell her. "If he really wanted money he would move back to South America and live off his own family. Everything he does, he does for love," I say with sudden conviction.

"How do you know that?" she asks.

"He married Dana, didn't he?"

It doesn't really make sense but it sounds sort of mean so she laughs and says maybe I'm right.

At the airport they stand in a row. My sister, her hands on her hips, squares her shoulders and takes what I call her Wonder Woman stance. A couple with small children is staring. When my plane is announced we make a great show of saying goodbye, hugging and kissing each other lavishly, calling each other "My dear sister" and "My darling brother-in-law". I pick up my bag. "Kiss me!" I command them, and they start in again, flinging themselves at me. The young couple is amazed. We are satisfied. Then my mother gets distracted by a janitor cleaning out a nearby ashtray with a damp rag. Joey stands, straight and small, between her and my sister, dutifully attentive to my departure. I don't even have to look back to know that his dark eyes will remain fixed on me, and he will continue waving until I disappear through the doors. I do anyway, though, and blow them all another kiss.

They're surprised and grateful, and blow some back. For a minute I just stand there feeling proud of them.

AN INCIDENT

Ginger Darling rolled down the windows of her tomato red VW Rabbit and backed out of her space in the faculty parking lot of Adams State College. She remembered how she and Molly had laughed together when they bought this car. It would be good for her, Molly had told her, to own a diesel. She was so quiet. It would be good for her to make some noise. When she roared into the parking lot, people would think she was on a motorcycle.

Ginger reached up and smoothed her hair just like Molly had done earlier that day. After ten years of living together, Ginger still couldn't believe that Molly, a formerly married woman with two children, had chosen her as her life partner. But she had. And until today, everything had gone smoothly. The social barriers they had expected to find to their relationship had simply melted away as they approached them. It was like a miracle.

Until today. Ginger adjusted the rearview mirror again before pulling out of the lot, as if by getting just the right angle she would be able to see back into the afternoon's incident and rearrange it, erase it as easily as she had erased her blackboard at the end of class.

"The girl has a problem," Ginger reminded herself. "Not you."

Ginger yawned tensely. The first day of classes would have been difficult and exhausting anyway, even without the incident with Maria. It was always hard to get back into the rhythm of teaching. In the classroom, Ginger felt she was straining her vocal cords just to talk loud enough to be heard. The early autumn weather was hot and sticky, making the students fidget. The girls in the front row gave up trying to appear to be good students and audibly dug through their bags for their compact mirrors and lipstick, their pantyhose swishing as they crossed and recrossed their legs, while Ginger delivered her first mini-lesson on freewriting.

Back in her office, at long last, Ginger had leafed through a bedraggled pile of first-day compositions, hurriedly scribbled on pages yanked from spiral notebooks, fringe dangling from their edges. She had asked for a personal narrative about an incident that had changed the writer's life. "The thing that really changed my life," she read, "was the time we went to Disney World. First we took the plane to Orlando, Florida." Ginger took off her glasses and rubbed her eyes. She turned to another. "The best time I ever had was when me and Dad went hunting up in the Mount Greylock Reservation."

One of the repeating students, Maria Tomasco, had come up to her after class and asked for an appointment, explaining that she was worried because she didn't understand why she had failed the course last spring. Ginger had agreed to see her. The girl seemed troubled, eager to improve. As soon as the appointment was over, she had promised herself the reward of going home to work in her garden for an hour before turning to her first stack of student papers.

Maria arrived at three-fifteen for her three o'clock appointment. She was a sturdy girl dressed in a red tank top and khaki shorts, her thick black hair still damp from a shower.

"Volleyball practice already," she explained, pushing her hair out of her face. "Can you believe it?"

Ginger had invited her to sit down. She had glanced, but just for a moment, at Maria's long, muscular, golden legs.

"You've been on the beach this summer, haven't you," she said.

Long ago she had given herself permission for fleeting glances, for that occasional sinking in the pit of her stomach when one of her students was particularly beautiful. It helped her walk through the classroom door. It was harmless. She was much too old to be a real threat to them and anyway, male professors got away with such nonsense all the time.

Maria had great legs. She glanced at them again, for a split second, before Maria sat down at the long, low table Ginger had moved into her small office for the purpose of holding student writing conferences. She looked at Ginger with an expression that said, "Let's get this over with." Ginger sat down beside her, aware that they were both tightly squeezed into the small space between her desk and the cinder-block wall and that this arrangement might not be ideal. But this semester Ginger wanted to try sitting next to her students, rather than across from them, so that they could both look at the student's paper at the same time. She had learned this technique from a book on how to teach college writing she had read over the summer. With Maria, though, it felt wrong. Each time she looked up, she felt that her face was too close to Maria's. She pushed her chair back, away from the low wooden table and Maria, and as she did their knees bumped. Maria flinched and glared at Ginger's leg.

"Excuse me," Ginger told her. "Let's look at the introduction. I like your categories. But are you sure there are only three?" Maria had written a composition about lying, claiming that people lied for only three reasons: to get to know someone, to save face, or to avoid physical harm. It seemed familiar to Ginger, as if Maria had copied it from somewhere.

"My 099 teacher told me you're supposed to have three things in your introduction and then write a paragraph about each one," Maria explained.

"Well," Ginger began. "Okay. But this was supposed to be a narrative you know, a story with an introduction that serves to get the reader interested."

Maria's face was blank. This was obviously news to her.

"Let's just read through it and see what you've got that could be developed into the story of an incident that changed you."

They hunched over the table and Maria began to read aloud although she clearly did not want to. As she read, she ran her hand through her thick black curls over and over again.

"You see, Maria," Ginger said.

Maria raked her hand through her hair again. Ginger was distracted by her gesture and forgot what she was saying. Without even thinking, as if she were talking to one of Molly's children, Ginger reached over and took hold of Maria's hand and said, "Could you stop doing that, please?"

Maria was immediately on her feet.

"Hey," she said. "Lay off, okay?"

"I'm sorry," Ginger said, also standing. "I just ..."

Maria looked disgusted, as if Ginger had reached over and slipped her hand up under the long loose leg of her khaki shorts.

"Look," Maria said, packing up her papers. "I didn't mind coming in here and talking to you about my composition I mean it was giving me the creeps the way you sit so close and all ..." Her mouth quivered. "But from now on you leave the door open. With all of us. Or I'm telling."

"Wait," Ginger said, reaching for her arm, realizing from the girl's expression that she was making another major mistake.

"Quit it, you old dyke. I'm warning you."

"I've been in a monogamous relationship for ten years," Ginger said, surprising them both.

Maria thought for a moment.

"That don't mean shit," she said, and she left.

Replaying this scene in her mind, Ginger drove through the center of town, past the white clapboard Congregational Church with its tall steeple. Last Sunday she and Molly had walked through those doors together, with Molly's ten-year-old son, Justin, trailing behind. Ginger could feel the approving looks of the members of the congregation who were already seated on the dark red cushions in the white-painted pews. Leslie, Molly's daughter, preferred to sit in the back with her best friend, Janice. Ginger sometimes heard them giggling during the sermon.

It seemed incredible to her, but no one really seemed to mind that she and Molly were a couple. Rich, the minister, had said more than once, in public, that they had one of the most stable relationships he had ever encountered and that no one in his church was ever going to say that their kind of love was wrong. The congregation had actually applauded. As she drove by, Ginger murmured a brief prayer. "Please God, don't let her make something of this."

If only she hadn't touched her, Ginger thought again, banging her fist lightly on the steering wheel. No one would believe anything bad of her, if only she hadn't let her flesh come into contact with the girl's. She would not be able to deny this. She would not lie. But what had she been thinking of? Even Leslie didn't want to be touched anymore, not by anyone. She had not been thinking. That's what she would say to anyone who asked. And someone surely would. Since the new Sexual Harassment Committee had been founded last spring at the college, headed by

Barbara Brody, an ardent feminist in the Math Department who was extremely uncomfortable around Ginger, Maria would certainly register a complaint. Since last spring it seemed that every girl on campus thought of herself as another Anita Hill. Ginger didn't know what the procedure was. Would they notify her in writing? Would her department chair call her into his office?

When she had almost reached her house, Ginger turned left instead of right. She was not ready to go home yet. She drove on and pulled into the "U-Pick" parking lot at Worthington Farms.

"I'll be all right," she said aloud, as if someone had inquired about her condition after she had taken a fall.

She stopped to look at the sheep. They raised their slender black faces toward her, curious, their jaws moving from side to side as they chewed. She took a step closer. Their chewing stopped. Silly animals, Ginger thought. She took another step toward them and a shiver of fear went through the flock. Then, ashamed of herself, she walked on, taking the path into the woods. She could see deer tracks in the red, deeply eroded earth. She trudged up the hill, slipping in her good shoes, the ground squishy beneath her feet from the thunderstorms of the weekend. The mud on the path where the water had recently evaporated looked as smooth as skin. A swarm of flies hovered over it. The brook gliding between the rocks moved thickly, as if it had the consistency of blood, not water.

She was sweating and wished she had left the jacket of her skirt suit in the car. A deer fly buzzed loudly around her head. She felt the small wings of another insect fluttering on her neck. Ginger swatted and kept walking. She would go to the top of the hill, take a good look at the view of the surrounding farms and a deep breath, and be herself again. She would stop worrying. She had done nothing wrong.

After she crossed the bridge over the Westfield River, Ginger took the path up to Windago Hill, used mostly by hunters and trappers. It went through a grove of hemlock, then to a clearing. As she turned onto it, the path became both narrower and steeper. The shadows were cool. She stopped for a moment to catch her breath.

Ginger closed her eyes and tried to picture the next day. What came into her mind was like a scene from a made-for-TV movie. A group of young men sprawl in their seats. The professor walks in. One boy leans over to whisper something in another

An Incident

one's ear. The whole group snickers. The professor nervously adjusts her blouse and begins her lecture. From the back of the room, someone hurls a projectile which grazes her left temple. She pretends not to notice.

Suddenly, Ginger wanted very badly to go home. She wanted to talk to Molly. Later, after the kids were in bed, she could tell Molly what had happened. Molly would take her hand and look into her eyes and say something like, "Poor thing. How terrible for you," and she would feel much better. She tried to imagine what Molly would have done in her place. She would be understanding. She would not panic. Molly was the kind of woman who inspired confidence, anyway. She was a nurse at the high school and her office was always crowded with kids wanting to tell her their secrets. Just the other day, another boy had come out to her.

"I think that's wonderful," she had told him. "I think it's great that you know who you are and what you want and you're ready to stop pretending."

The boy had burst into tears of gratitude.

Molly would have opened the door to her office, sat down calmly, and said to Maria. "There. The door is open. Now can we talk about why you're so angry?"

As she walked back down the hill toward the car, Ginger was assaulted by another image from a grade B movie. This time she was slouching out of the building toward the parking lot. Just as she reached her car, she was surrounded by boys in football jackets, Maria's boyfriend among them. "Well, fellas," she said, trying to appear calm. "What can I do for you?" One of them would push her in the back with his flattened palm. "Well, bulldagger," he would say. "Can't keep your hands off the girls, huh?"

"Don't be ridiculous, "Ginger told herself, starting the car. But she was not completely convinced that something like this couldn't happen at Adams State.

At home, Ginger stepped out of her muddy shoes, leaving them on the threadbare green carpet in the front hall. She leafed through the small pile of bills on the front hall table, aware that she was trying to behave as if nothing had happened. She could hear the tinny sound of the Anderson's television set, tuned to the six o'clock news, through the open dining room windows, and the

An Incident

deeper sound of the backbeat from Leslie's stereo, coming through the floorboards from upstairs.

Justin was sitting on the sofa, a photo album open on his lap. "Hey, Ginge," he said. "You wanna look at some more pictures?"

To Justin, the photographs of his summer at camp were endlessly fascinating. He was always eager for Ginger to look at them with him.

"Sure," Ginger told him. "In a minute."

The orange cat trotted out from the kitchen and flopped on its back, hoping to be stroked. Ginger stepped over it and padded across the wooden floor and onto the cool linoleum in her stocking feet. She needed Molly.

Molly was standing at the counter, her thin pale hair falling down over her shoulders, her right hand moving rhythmically. Water was boiling on the stove, making the lid of the saucepan jangle. Beyond her, through the window, the Anderson boy was in his backyard, throwing a bright pink frisbee for his small black and white dog to retrieve. Ginger slid her arms around Molly's waist, comforted by the soft roll of flesh she dressed so carefully to conceal, by the heaviness of her breasts on her arms. A cool breeze blew through the window onto her face. The cat rubbed against the backs of her legs.

"How was your day?" Molly stroked Ginger's cheek, her hand pungent with onions, and pressed her soft lips against Ginger's. "Did it come right back to you? Was it like riding a bicycle?"

Molly had started a week earlier than Ginger and had already gone through what she called "decompression."

"It was okay," Ginger said, holding Molly tightly. "I've got a big pile of papers to read," she added, as if that were her only problem.

"We can eat in about ten minutes," Molly told her, disengaging herself from Ginger's embrace and turning back to the counter. "Why don't you call Leslie and ask her to set the table?"

Ginger walked halfway up the stairs, took a deep breath and hollered, "Leslie, could you set the table?"

She didn't go all the way up and knock on her door. Leslie considered that a major intrusion. The next time, she thought, when she needed to remind herself how to behave toward a student, male or female, she would use Leslie as a model. She had

An Incident

trained herself to be very careful around Leslie. "*Les*lee!" she yelled again, not getting a response. "Time to set the *ta*ble!" Finally she opened her door, the loud music pouring out into the hallway from behind her.

"I *heard* you," she said.

"How could I know that?" Ginger asked her, genuinely puzzled.

"Oh, Ginger. Don't play dumb, okay? It's extremely irritating."

She went back into her room again, slamming the door behind her. She turned off the stereo and the house became abruptly silent.

Ginger sat down on the sagging yellow corduroy sofa beside Justin and hugged him tightly, grateful that he was only ten years old and untainted by puberty. Justin hugged her back, then jabbed her in the ribs.

"Look," he said. "My first swan dive."

Leslie flounced downstairs and into the kitchen. Dishes clattered onto the counter. Between her and Molly, it was even worse. A friend with older children had told them that once their kids were past twenty, it was clear sailing again. Five more years of this, then, Ginger thought.

How horrible it would be for Leslie, for all of them, if this incident with Maria became public, if Leslie's friends at school learned that Ginger had been accused of molesting a teenaged girl. Ginger knew the cruelty of teenagers. She could imagine very clearly how Leslie's friends would torment her, how they would ask if she weren't afraid of being mauled by her mother's lover.

Ginger stared at the photos Justin was showing her, paralyzed with fear. What if the newspapers got hold of it? Could Molly lose the custody of her children? Justin was under twelve, too young, according to the courts, to decide for himself where he wanted to live. Molly spoke often of how relieved she would be when he could speak for himself. He had known no other parents than Molly and Ginger and was totally devoted to them. But he wasn't twelve yet. There was still time for their lives to be shattered by this.

She has seen newspaper reports ruin the lives of two people in town. One was Jeff Christian, the dentist on River Road, whose family had woken up one morning to the headline, *SEX RX*, an article about an affair he had with one of his patients. He had the affair, of course, and deserved to be blamed, but the newspaper had blown it way out of proportion. And then there was poor Joan Stevens, accused by a part-time instructor of not rehiring him because he had withdrawn his "sexual favors" from her. He had gone to the local paper with the story. They had a field day.

"I'll be right back, pal," Ginger said to Justin and went up the slippery wooden stairs to the bedroom she shared with Molly, thinking it might be better if she fell and broke her neck than if Maria went public. She went into the room and closed the door, feeling weak in the knees and near tears. She began changing out of her work clothes, her "lady outfit," as Molly called it, and into her cutoffs and a T-shirt, when she caught sight of the photograph on the wall.

It was as if she were seeing it for the first time. Ten years ago, before they had officially gotten together, Molly had wanted desperately to fly to Seattle and show her brother her new baby. But she had just gotten divorced and didn't have enough money. Ginger had suggested taking the train and called to find out the price of tickets, but it was still much too expensive. That was when she had her brainstorm.

"What about families? Don't you have some kind of family excursion fare?"

"Well, why didn't you tell me you were a family, ma'am?" the railroad clerk had said, suddenly affable.

They had traveled across America as a family. Ginger had dressed as a man, in sunglasses, a large, loose jacket, and a mustache that a gay friend in the theater had taught her to paste on, hair by hair. Molly said she looked just like a British rock star. She spent much of the trip in silence, her voice too high to be any man's, with six-month-old Justin on her lap and Leslie sitting beside her, enthralled by this wonderful new version of dress-up. Molly's brother had found this hilarious and had brought his camera to the railroad station when he came to pick them up. Molly had the picture enlarged and had hung it on their bedroom wall, claiming that it was during this trip she had truly fallen in love with Ginger because she had been willing to make such a sacrifice to be with her.

Ginger stood close and peered at the picture, imagining how it would look on the front page of the newspaper. *LESBO PROF IN DRAG MAULS COED* the headline would read.

An Incident

Molly called them to the table. She had made steamed vegetables with two dipping sauces and cold cuts for supper. It was too hot to turn the stove on for long, she explained apologetically, mostly to Leslie, who had recently become a fussy eater as well. The half gallon of ice cream in the freezer would take care of Justin. Ginger sat down at the head of the table and looked at Molly's rumpled children. Justin's hair stuck out in all directions because he hadn't combed it. Leslie's did because she took large armfuls from one side of her head and tossed them over to the other side. Ginger made a silent promise to God to stop coloring her hair if she wasn't publicly accused of being a homosexual who tried to molest girls. It seemed like a feeble promise. She would have to come up with something better.

Ginger reached out for the children's hands to say grace. Justin's hand was sticky. Leslie's was warm and smooth and given unwillingly. Ginger looked down at the table, chips of varnish missing from its edges, and the bowls of steaming vegetables.

"Dear God," she said. "Make us truly thankful for what we are about to receive."

The telephone rang.

"I'll get it!" Leslie said, pushing back her chair.

"I'll get it," Ginger told her. They had rules. One of them was that Leslie was not allowed to have long, whispered phone conversations with her girlfriends during dinner.

She picked up the phone.

"Hello?"

"Hello, Ginger. Is this a bad time for you?"

It was Jim Briggs, the chair of the English Department.

"We just sat down to dinner, Jim," Ginger told him, because that was the family rule. "Can I call you back?"

"No need. Just stop by my office before your first class tomorrow."

Ginger felt as if an enormous hand were squeezing her chest, making it impossible for her to breathe or talk.

"Anything wrong?" she managed to squeak out.

"No, no. Marianne Withrow has a scheduling conflict. We thought you might be able to juggle things a little."

"Okay, fine," Ginger said. "No problem."

"Thanks, Ginger," Jim told her. "I knew I could count on you. We'll talk tomorrow."

Ginger hung up the phone and stood looking out the kitchen window toward the Anderson's house, waiting for her breathing to become regular again. She could hear that her family had started without her. The three Andersons were sitting in their kitchen, having supper too. A rectangle of pale yellow light fell from their window on the lawn between the two houses. In the center of the rectangle was a large, gray squirrel, squat and heavy, perched precariously in the Anderson's squirrel-proof bird feeder, eating up the seed.

"Everything okay?" Molly called to her.

"Fine," Ginger said, returning to the table and sitting down. "Everything's fine."

LOVE STORIES

Kevin comes in, his red bathing suit still damp, his eyes glazed over. He has been smoking dope with Larry again, down by the clay cliffs. His thick dark hair is disheveled, as if he has just gotten up from a nap. He lingers in the doorway, one hand on his hip, as if unable to decide if he wants to come in or not.

The screen door slaps shut behind him. Outside, the scrub pines hunch on the edge of the lawn and the sun shines golden as it nears the horizon. Bobby and I are sitting in the small room off the kitchen that should be a sun porch but isn't. There are windows on three sides but they're not large enough. Still, it's the brightest room in the house.

We are visiting our friend, Ann, on Martha's Vineyard. Ann gave up a tenure track position as an assistant professor of Anthropology at the same university we teach for to work as the cook in a health food store here. We can't decide if she's lost her mind or if she's the only one of us with any sense. We whisper about her when she leaves the room and watch her carefully the rest of the time. She frowns a lot and shoves the furniture around. She puts her glass of Scotch down so hard that some of it leaps up and spills onto the table, seeping into the old wood. But she's always been a heavy drinker.

Ann is in the kitchen, near enough to participate in our conversation if she raises her voice a little, and she does. She is like that.

Bobby and I are drinking beer. I don't usually drink beer before the sun sets, but it's the first day of my summer vacation and Jackie isn't with me and I'll do whatever I damn well please.

Whenever Kevin comes into the room, Bobby goes limp. He slouches, one arm tossed nonchalantly over the back of his chair, as if he has just turned into a rag doll. His legs are apart, his feet resting on their outside edges, the way a baby's would if you sat it up. I don't understand what this means. Kevin has the opposite reaction. He is like a cat when another cat enters his territory. He arches his back and bristles. They both claim to like each other very much.

"So how is Larry?" Bobby asks, slouching. "Eager to please as ever?"

Eventually, almost everyone becomes the butt of one of our jokes, but for the moment, Larry is our favorite. First of all, we met him because I met his ex-wife, Brenda, at a benefit for The Gay and Lesbian Community Center in Manhattan. Brenda's a minister now. She specializes in commitment ceremonies for couples of lesbians and gay men and spent the party telling us in her somber, self-righteous way how a commitment before God was even better than one before the law. She strode around the room with her hands folded behind her, talking about C.S. Lewis and the four loves.

Brenda had given us Larry's phone number when she heard we were coming up here to visit Ann. Larry invited us over for bluefish and the sunset, and by the end of the evening his pudgy sunburned hand was resting on Kevin's thigh while he whispered about his infidelities to Brenda. Kevin plucked Larry's hand off as if it were a spider. But then they started getting stoned together sort of regularly and the more they got stoned together, the more Larry revealed about his sordid past. Nowadays he just drives back and forth to Vineyard Haven, picking up hitchhikers.

"You can't tell me she didn't know," Ann says, disgusted. "I don't believe she didn't know what he was doing. They probably weren't even sleeping together, right?"

"I doubt it, " Kevin says, looking closely at the back of his hand, studying his fingernails. His face is so large and pale it is like the moon has come in the window. I push back my chair on the old linoleum, feeling like I have to catch my breath.

Ann is making her famous spaghetti sauce. Her apron and the wall beside the stove are covered with reddish-orange flecks. She pushes her graying hair away from her face with her forearm. There are flecks of sauce, like freckles, on her cheeks and neck. Ann became a good cook when she was married to a man who was in the State Department and gave dinner parties for fifty.

Larry confessed to Kevin that while he was married to Brenda, the now-minister, he went on rampages in Central Park, wandering drunk and disoriented on drugs through the Ramble, getting laid by anyone who would have him.

Kevin touches his temple with one finger, then brushes his hair back, gently, as if it were spun glass and could fall to the floor and shatter.

"She probably knew," he says. Then looks at me. "Somebody tell a story. Somebody tell about a ruined relationship."

They want me to tell about Julia again. Julia, the Colombian girl in my Listening/Speaking class. There is a thrill that goes through us when I tell this story because they all know that I have told each of them, separately, more than I've ever told when we are all together. Nobody knows what it's safe to mention. Kevin doesn't know if Bobby has heard about the time when we were alone together on the fire stairs at the college and Julia pushed herself against me. Ann doesn't know if I told either of them about the evening I let Julia drive me home.

It was summer but I was shivering. I couldn't stop my teeth from chattering. "I feel so good when I'm near you," she said. I looked her over, doing inventory, my teeth clattering around in my head: thick black wavy hair, dark liquid eyes, smooth olive skin, high firm breasts. How old was she? Twenty? Twenty two?

"I don't know," she said. "My English. Is it right what I say?"

"Right? You mean correct English?"

She stopped at a red light and turned to look at me.

"I think I mean right like okay with you."

"I think I'm supposed to say no," I told her. She was my student. We had the same first name. It felt wrong.

She reached over and stroked my cheek.

"Don't say no," she said.

I thought of other stories we could tell but would rather not: Ann could tell about allowing herself to be seduced by the same man who had seduced her secretary. Bobby could tell about the hitchhiker who had knifed him and the real story about what he had done to deserve it. Kevin could remind us about the period of his life when he stood at the ironing board in his chenille robe, slightly off the shoulder, and waited all afternoon for Carlos to come home from the party he had gone to the night before. I could tell about Jackie discovering me making out in the car with Julia. But we all liked to think we have gotten beyond that.

"I have a new one for you," Bobby says, smiling maliciously. "I have a new episode in the lives of Joye and Eddie."

Ann puts down the wooden spoon she is using to stir the sauce in the deep cast iron pot. She is interested.

I feel nervous. I haven't been able to forget the last time Bobby told us a story. It was about Roy, his colleague at the college where he used to teach before he was denied tenure, a stunned-looking blond man with the face of a chronic drinker.

Roy went to his favorite bar, The Monster, and, as usual, had too much to drink because it was Christmas break, and he always has too much to drink when he is off from teaching. On this particular evening Roy met a young blond man with a moustache. He especially likes men who look like him—this is what Bobby said—and got very drunk and invited him home. Bobby didn't give us a lot of details about what happened next, but he said that the moment came when the man had Roy tied up with the telephone wire and was holding a knife to his throat but then he kissed him and walked out the door. It was the next day that Roy saw one of those police drawings of the guy in the newspaper. *MYSTERY MAN PREYS ON GAYS* the headline said, and the article told that he had already been seen leaving bars with three men who had later been found dead, their throats slit.

When Bobby starts talking about Joye and Eddie, I begin to pick at the loose paint chips on the edge of the table. Bobby has narrow shoulders and a pouchy gut and his legs are as white as the face of a woman from another century who never goes out in the sun. He is wearing a striped T-shirt that's a little too small and a pair of long baggy shorts with a lot of pockets. He eats a couple of potato chips, heaping on the dip and opening his mouth wide, before he begins to talk. Ann sits down at the table with us. She and Sharon broke up three years ago, and she hasn't met anyone else. It's not that she's too old. She just can't decide what she wants.

"Well," Bobby says, running his hand gingerly over the top of his head where he has been dabbing chemicals and is no longer bald. "You know they met on the street."

"I don't know anything," Kevin says. "Start at the beginning."

Bobby leans back in his chair, just at the sound of Kevin's voice. Is this like a cat rolling over on its back?

Love Stories

"You know that Joye has to be involved with someone who doesn't want her. The last man she was with was married."

"There's nothing unusual about that," Ann says, already losing interest.

"Okay. Wait. So one recent summer evening she's walking her dog --not the little white one that yipped, but this new large one she's got. She's walking her dog in Central Park, and she strikes up a conversation with this Italian guy. I mean very Italian with the unbuttoned shirt, the hairy chest, the gold chains, the tatoo, the whole bit."

"That *is* unusual," Ann mutters, "for her."

"So she ends up bringing him home, and they start up this very hot relationship."

"The same night?" I ask. "Whatever happened to safe sex?"

Bobby laughs.

"Exactly," he says. "But, as you know, I'm in no position to judge. So if Joye wants to get involved with an Italian who is ten years younger than she is, has no education, and doesn't work, that's her business. The only thing is I keep noticing that there's something a little unusual about him. I mean he seems to be as interested in me as he is in Joye."

Ann snorts.

"Oh, Bobby," she says. "You think that about every boy you meet."

Bobby sits up, laughing.

"No!" he says. "Wait. Listen to this. So we go out together, the three of us, in the West Village and the new guy, Eddie, starts talking about the gay bars like he knows them really well. He says, 'They don't let women into The Monster unless they're lesbians.' Things like that. Things you wouldn't know unless you'd been inside a lot."

"So maybe he's bisexual," Ann says. "What's wrong with that?"

Ann has taken a turn at every sexual identity, so it's almost impossible to have a conversation without offending her.

Bobby ignores this remark and goes on.

"I start questioning Joye when Eddie isn't around. What does he do for a living. Who else does he spend his time with? Things like that. She tells me he doesn't seem to work at all but he always has large amounts of cash. Then she tells me the whole story."

He reaches for another potato chip, loads it with dip, puts it in his mouth and chews. Bobby takes his time chewing. There is no way any one of us is going to change the subject.

"It turns out that Eddie has a friend. A male friend," Bobby says, raising his eyebrows significantly. "They have been friends for ten years. The friend is older. He takes Eddie on vacations to Key West. But they're just friends, Joye says. For Christmas, he gave Eddie a mink jacket from Bergdorf Goodman, but they're just friends." Bobby looks from one to the other of us, pleased with the incredulity on our faces.

"Of course they are," Kevin says, very blasé. "I was going to give you a mink jacket for your birthday, Bobby. Now you've spoiled the surprise."

The sun has set and the shapes of the trees are disappearing. Bobby tilts his head back and finishes off his beer. Ann gets up to get him another one. Bobby is the fastest drinker among us.

"The worst part is what happened at Eddie's mother's house when it was his birthday. Eddie's mother likes the boyfriend—you don't mind if I call him that, do you?—better than she likes Joye. If she had to choose between them, she'd choose the boyfriend. He has money. He buys *her* gifts, too."

Kevin pushes back his chair, making a loud scraping noise on the floor, startling all of us. But he doesn't get up, and Bobby continues.

"So Eddie, intelligent young man that he is, decides to invite both Joye and the boyfriend to his birthday party at Mom's. There's a cake. The mother and all the brothers and sisters are there. At one point in the evening the boyfriend pulls Joye aside and snarls at her, 'You want him? *You* pay his credit card bills."

"How do you know this?" Ann says, suddenly drunk and in her mood to doubt everything.

"Joye *told*," Bobby says smugly.

Ann starts to get up to check her sauce.

"Wait," Bobby says. "There's more."

One corner of his mouth is pulled back, as if someone had hooked him like a fish and were yanking on the line.

She sits down again.

"Later that evening, when everyone has had too much to drink, the old queen pulls Joye aside again and is in the middle of calling her a broken-down old slut—Joye at least has the presence of mind to say, 'Look who's talking!'—when Eddie walks by and overhears him. So Eddie hauls off and slugs the guy. And all the other party guests, including the mother—this is Eddie's birthday party, remember—pretend like nothing is happening. The boyfriend ends up in the emergency room with three broken ribs, and Eddie has to stay over at his house for several days afterwards to take care of him."

"So does Joye finally see the light after this?" I ask him.

"No," Bobby says. "She thinks Eddie was defending her honor. She thinks they've never had a fight like this before."

"I feel sorry for her," Ann says, getting up heavily and going back to the stove. "Shall I put the pasta in?" she yells, unnecessarily loud. "Is anyone hungry?"

No one answers but she puts it in anyway. I go out on the lawn to see if the moon has come up yet. It has. I want to call Jackie. I imagine that if I describe where I am and how much I want her, she'll forgive me. I imagine her agreeing to get on a plane in the morning, the two of us spending the day on the beach.

But I know it's just the beer talking.

Inside the house, Kevin and Bobby sit at the table as still as statues.

THE DUCHESS

I go around the corner to The Duchess about three times a week. Who am I kidding? Exactly three times a week. On Sundays after ten. And on Wednesdays and Thursdays I walk up from my lousy job as the only "administrative assistant" to these three jokers who sell surplus parts on Canal Street and go right in and have a few beers without even going home first.

I don't go near the place on Friday and Saturday nights when the kids from Queer Nation take over. It's too depressing. I'm too old. Who needs it? On Fridays and Saturdays I rent a video or two, buy myself a six-pack and a couple slices of pizza, and try to learn how to be my own best friend. By Sunday evening

I've had it with keeping myself company and am back at the bar again.

Before we broke up, my ex, Monica, explained that you have to be really good-looking—like she is. She didn't say this but it was implied—to meet someone in a bar. Either that or you have to have terrific breasts. Otherwise, who would notice you? Why would anyone even see you through the smoke, through the thick crowd of women's bodies? Why would anyone squeeze her way through the crowd to ask you to dance if it didn't seem worth it? No reason at all. That's what Monica was telling me. I've got absolutely nothing that would make another woman slide down off her bar stool and come over to ask me to dance. I have to do all the sliding and walking and asking. I'm aware of that. I know what my options are. Do the walking or don't get any.

Lately, since Monica and I broke up, I haven't been doing much but looking and trying to stay out of trouble. It doesn't mean I don't go to the bar, but I don't ask anyone to dance much. I'm waiting until I'm sure I can trust myself again. After what happened with Monica, I don't want to rush into anything new.

Last week, though, I started chatting with a small squat woman with very short red hair—she was almost bald-looking.

The Duchess

She was sitting on the stool next to mine, and I was looking at her severe hairdo thinking that my own hair could use a trim, that I'm starting to grow little wings out of the sides of my head. When I'm not trying to pick a woman up, I have no trouble at all starting a conversation. I had ordered a Bud Lite and settled in for another evening of getting my clothes stunk up with cigarette smoke and stained with the drinks women were going to spill on me as they tried to squeeze between me and the woman next to me to order, when the bald-headed woman, whose name was Lucy, and I just sort of struck up a conversation. I wished I could have taken out a piece of paper and written the beginning down for later when I'm trying to pick up one of the pretty ones and am all tongue-tied. Anyway, I was thinking so hard, trying to replay the conversation in my mind, "What'd she say?" "What'd I say?" that it wasn't until old Lucy laid her freckled hand on my arm and said she was sure she had seen me somewhere before that I realized she was trying to pick me up. Right away I started to feel that familiar ache between my thighs. This embarrasses me a little.

Lucy asked me if I wanted to dance—just get up and shuffle around a little, was how she put it. It was a fast song. I thought that was sort of cute and decided to cut myself a little slack. With Lucy, dancing didn't seem dangerous. She wasn't one of those types I have to watch out for. She was dressed in an old flannel shirt and had a really sad expression in her eyes, like she had had more than her fair share of hard times with women, too. I was telling myself that maybe we could just go back to the tiny dance floor where several couples were already jostling each other like billiard balls and the smoke was hanging like fog from the ceiling, the star-making machine was twirling, that Lucy and I could just grind it up a little on the dance floor, no harm done, a little kissing, maybe, a stray hand sliding down her thigh. But then I caught sight of her butt. Lucy looked like she had a pantload of cottage cheese. Too bad because her face was pretty. But I sat right down on my stool again and said thank you I was comfortable where I was. Monica used to say that with looks like mine, I had no right to be so fussy. I told her that as long as I could get what I wanted, I was going to go on being as fussy as I damn well pleased.

After I turned her down, Lucy's shoulders tensed and her hands bunched up, but then she took a deep breath and started chatting again, as if it were no big deal. This is what I need to learn how to do.

The Duchess

On Thursdays, I get there early, sometimes around five-thirty or so, and watch the place fill up with women. It's like being the first one at the beach and then getting surrounded by bodies. Before you know it, there are women everywhere you look. Lately they seem to have a new position they like. This sounds like I'm talking about sex, but I'm not. What happens is that one woman sits on a stool with her back against the bar and her partner or whatever you want to call her (I prefer girlfriend) backs up to her, and then the one on the stool wraps herself around her, arms and legs. Like any minute the one standing up is going to take off with her girlfriend on her back, piggy-back style. To them this seems romantic. Who am I to judge?

A woman with thick dark hair down to her waist, hair that makes her hold her head very still and get a sort of arrogant look on her face, has squeezed between me and the woman on the next stool three times already. I could reach right out and pat her butt if I wanted to. It's cute enough. I don't do that sort of thing. Also, I have the feeling that she would put up with it in a way that would be insulting to me. What I mean is, she would smile indulgently, thinking of me as harmless, the way nurses treat little old men in wheelchairs who grab at them.

Each time the girl squeezes in—she's wearing a tight black sweater and black jeans and cut off cowboy boots, a totally familiar outfit—Lee, the barmaid, rushes right over to serve her, dropping everything. Lee and I used to have the kind of relationship that consisted of rolling our eyes at each other when somebody got loud and giving each other knowing looks when somebody was putting on the make. She is also likely to yell out, "Keep it clean, girls! This is a family bar!" She is from the Midwest and when she does this, it's convincing, and for a moment there's an awful hush that comes over the place. The women look at each other, bewildered, like they're asking each other, "How did somebody's mother get in here?" Then everybody starts laughing when they realize it's just Lee.

Right after she heard about what happened between me and Monica, Lee started keeping away from my end of the bar unless I called her over to order another beer. She brings me my beer and I am grateful for that, since there's a sign hanging over the bar that says, "We reserve the right to refuse to serve anyone for any reason." But she won't talk to me or even look at me anymore.

"What can I get you, sweetheart?" Lee asks the girl.

"My name is Chloe," says the girl with long hair in a snotty tone, "and I'd like a Rusty Nail."

"Coming right up," Lee says, nonplussed. She's the kind of person you wish you'd had for a best friend in high school. She would have calmed you down when you were itching for a brawl.

This Chloe is just a kid. They probably checked her ID at the door. A kid with long shiny hair which she pats and fluffs like she brought her Persian cat along to the bar with her. This hair of hers sets off red flashing lights in my head, like being pulled over by a state trooper. Monica, too, spent too much time and energy fussing over her hair, which was thick and wild and auburn, the way you'd expect someone with her name's hair to be. She would be looking in the mirror, fixing it, fussing, fussing, fussing with her hair, tying it up, letting it down, fluffing it ... oh so preoccupied, while I'd be standing behind her, the cords in my neck bulging, shouting about how she was torturing me, making me feel like an animal. She did not even turn around. She looked at my image beside hers in the mirror and talked to that, as if that were doing the yelling. I tried to restrain myself. I really did. This went on for a long time before I finally broke down and let her have it.

Chloe is standing right next to me. I can feel her hipbone pressing against my waist. She is going to keep standing there, her skinny body pressed against the bar, watching Lee work. It doesn't matter since I am definitely not interested in her at all, and I have to go pee.

"Sit down for a minute if you want," I tell her. "I have to go downstairs."

"Thanks," she says, unnecessarily grateful.

When I come back upstairs, Chloe is perched, tentative as a sparrow, on my stool. She watches eagerly as I squeeze through the groups of hefty women gathered near the bar.

"Do you want to dance?" she asks before I get to say a word.

She is tall and very thin. The kind of girl who spends her whole life dreaming of being a model, the kind of thin, frail, pretty girl you could pick up and toss into your bed. Her hands are long and slender and her bony knees protrude through her tight jeans. I could hold both of her wrists in one hand.

The Duchess

She is waiting for an answer. I nod.

On the dance floor she is reserved at first. I try to pull her closer and she resists a little, as if she were saying *maybe*. Not *no* exactly, but *maybe*. Her skinny body, her ribs and shoulder blades feel tense, uncertain, like she's not sure she's safe. Then a fast song comes on. We dance and dance and dance.

By ten o'clock our bodies are soaked with sweat. Chloe shyly takes my hand and slips it up under her sweater and onto her bare back to show me how wet it is. Meanwhile the strobe light flashes and the room seems to whirl, and the other couples keep right on dancing. We start up again and before long it's like we are all tumbling around together in a giant cocktail mixer and I am not even thinking. I have switched from beer to straight Scotch to beer again. Lee keeps serving me the drinks. I don't even look up when I hand her the money. I watch the dollars go from my hand to hers and that's it. I know that if I looked up at her, she would give me a look that said, "I'm watching you," or "I'm thinking about warning your new girlfriend," so I keep my eyes down.

At midnight the songs on the jukebox get slow. This is a kind of tradition at the Duchess. After midnight on week nights we all start to slow down and face the fact that we have to go back to work the next morning. Chloe takes off her sweater and doesn't hold her body away from mine anymore. Her breasts are round and firm and press against mine in a way that makes me want to lift her thin cotton undershirt right up and put my mouth on them. As we sway to the music I take hold of her waist and pull her close and begin, very slowly, to move my hands. I can feel her ribs under my fingers, and I start sliding my hands forward, and she is not saying no. She is letting me put my hand up onto her breast, right there on the dance floor. I push my face into her neck and smell her sweet flesh and want much more of her. I am so surprised by her willingness that I can hardly remember what to do. By the time it comes back to me, her hand shoots up and drags mine back down to her waist and she whispers, "Not here." And in spite of all my promises to myself, I whisper back, "Where, then?"

She pushes me away from her, gently, almost as if she pities me for how much I want her, how easy it's going to be to bring me to my knees.

"I'm not ready for that yet," she says with a sweet smile. "Could we just dance for now?"

"Okay," I tell her, trying to seem cool and composed although my breath is coming out in gasps. "No problem."

I pull her back to me and we dance and I don't try anything again.

"Be grateful," I instruct myself, "that she doesn't want to move in tonight and begin a long term monogamous relationship."

Lee is yelling, "Last call." I go back to my stool and sit down. Tomorrow at work I am going to feel like hell. Suddenly it doesn't seem worth it.

"Let's sit this one out," I tell her.

"But it's the last song," she says, pleading. "They're going to unplug the jukebox." She seems like she might start to cry.

"I'm tired," I tell her. "I need a rest."

I order my Scotch and beer at the same time. She sits down beside me, brooding. She tosses her hair over her shoulders angrily now, as if it were a package she was tired of carrying. Then she gets up. We say goodnight. No phone numbers. No, "Are you sure you wouldn't like to come over?"

Then, on Friday morning, in the middle of typing a dumbass memo, my head pounding, I start feeling like a damn fool. What if she never comes back? What if I never see her again? She was vain and all, but for God's sake we were practically doing it on the dance floor and I didn't even get her phone number.

There is no way I'm going to wait until Sunday, either. Friday night or not, at eight, before they start charging a cover, I'm back in The Duchess again, pretending not to be looking for her.

When she comes in, she walks right up to me, like she knew I would be there. She tosses her long hair over her shoulders and says, "Let's dance," like she owns me or something. She has a dark green silk blouse on. I see that her nipples are hard, and I slide right down off my barstool and out onto the dance floor.

This time, though, I am the one who holds back when the slow songs start. I am the one who waits, who resists, who says, "Maybe." Chloe holds me tighter, pulls me closer, her strong lean thighs parting over one of mine, her body swooping down to rub against the coarse fabric of my jeans.

Then images of the last time with Monica start filling up my mind. I try to push them away, but they won't let me. I keep seeing it, again and again, Monica's shocked expression, the glass shattering, the way she tried to protect her face by holding up her forearms, her bleeding forearms, the floor slick with beer, my knees soaked with beer from when I slipped, the handful of her hair that I found in my pocket, much later, when I was out walking, out praying she would have the sense to pack up and get out before I came home again.

"Can I walk you home?" Chloe asks.

I am tempted to say no. I am strong enough to refuse her now, and it would be just what she needed to keep her interested. But I am trying to be good. I am trying to behave like a normal person. I tell her okay, I would like that.

We stand in the raw cold on the steep red steps in front of my apartment building, leaning against the shaky wrought iron railing. She is huddled up in her coat and would probably like to be invited in.

"Well, thanks," I tell her. I give her my most generous smile and touch her cheek with one finger. "See you."

"Tomorrow?" she says, stepping from one foot to the other, like a child. "Will you be there tomorrow?"

I feel a different kind of smile spreading across my face.

"Maybe," I tell her. "Maybe not."

"It's Saturday night. You must know if you're busy or not," she says, smiling. She likes this game.

"I do. I just don't know if it will be worth it or not for me to go into that smelly old bar again."

"It will be worth it," she says.

"Okay," I tell her. "Then I'll be there." And I turn and go up the stairs.

On Saturday I feel uneasy all day. I don't have the office to distract me. I don't have my three creepy bosses and their surplus supplies to get angry at. I cannot stop thinking about Chloe. I cannot. I try to go back to sleep, to read, to listen to the radio, to go for a walk, even watch a little daytime TV, but all I am doing is waiting for it to be night. I pace the floor of my apartment and watch the sky turn dark. I make myself some supper so I won't get drunk too fast. I even stand in front of my closet and worry about what I'm going to wear.

It is almost ten o'clock when she arrives. I have had two Scotches and several beers already, served by Lee, who gloats because I am there and I am alone. Chloe's face brightens when she sees me. All innocence.

"You're here!" she says, as if she's surprised. As if she did not make this whole thing happen. She checks her coat because it's very crowded with girls in spiky hairdos and leather and black tube skirts and big black shoes. She squeezes between me and the woman on the stool next to mine. I have on my silk blouse tonight. She is wearing a sweatshirt.

"You look beautiful," she says, then kisses me, for the first time, pressing her soft mouth onto mine.

"Let's dance," she says.

At four o'clock in the morning, when the bar closes, I am drunk and very steamed up. I invite her upstairs. What choice do I have? She sits down at the kitchen table and looks around but says nothing. There is nothing to say. It is not a nice apartment, and I have done nothing to make it nice. What was nice, Monica took with her.

I ask her if she wants another beer. She says yes, although her head must be spinning too. As I hand her the glass and bottle, the stuff with Monica looms up again. I push the images away. I close my eyes for a second. The room spins. Meanwhile, Chloe pours herself a glass of beer and moves over to the sofa. I can hear her doing this.

When I open my eyes she pats the place beside her. I don't even remember sitting down but then we are kissing, my tongue inside her mouth, and I am pushing her onto her back, not roughly but like I mean it, getting on top of her, prying her legs apart with one of mine. I kiss her neck, her throat, my mouth moving down toward her breasts. She is moaning a little, moving under me like she wants more. I start kissing her breast right through her undershirt, getting it drenched. I am lost now, completely. There is no going back from this. I reach down and unzip her jeans. With my other hand I take hold of one of her wrists, then the other one, and hold them, tight, over her head.

I was just going to slide my hand into her jeans and rest it there. I wasn't going to do anything. I was going to wait until she started to move, until she showed me what she wanted. But she must have gotten scared or something. Because suddenly she yanks herself away from me, pushes me off of her, then sits up, wild-eyed.

"What's going on?" she says.

I can hardly breathe. I can hardly believe what's going on inside my pants. It flashes through my mind that I could grab her hand and put it there and say, "This. This is what's going on."

I don't say anything. I sit very still and wait.

"I'm sorry," she says. "I haven't made love with a woman in a really long time." She gives me what she must think is a significant look. "I guess I'm not quite ready yet."

She gives my hand a little squeeze, then drinks down her beer. She stands and zips her pants. She goes into the kitchen, setting the empty glass on the table. I wait.

"I guess I should go now," she says.

I might have been all right. I might have been able to let her put on her coat and walk out the door.

But that isn't what she does. She stands in the middle of the kitchen, under the light, takes a mirror out of her bag and starts fixing her hair and checking her eye makeup. When she sees me coming toward her, she smiles.

SWIMMING IN WINTER

Maxine wiped the cold drizzle from her face, shaded her eyes and peered through the tinted glass. Mysteriously, the swimming pool was closed today. And yet she could see people walking around inside. She pulled on the door one last time, to be sure. The locker room attendant, dressed in his white uniform, was now coming over to tell her to go away.

"*Il faut pousser, mademoiselle,*" he said, pulling the door from his side, indicating that she should come in.

Maxine followed him sheepishly. Doors push *in* in France, she reminded herself. In America we are afraid of dying in fires but here doors go in. To them it seems logical.

She hurried into the locker room, hardly saying *bonjour* to the war veteran who sold pool passes. She went into a stall and took off her clothes, shoving them into the red plastic hamper provided by the attendant. She was ashamed, not only of being bewildered by the slightest difference between this city and home, but also because she had been up until three in the morning taking her frustration out on her husband, Paul. She had begun with a mild complaint about the narrowness of the sidewalks and the French women behind her, clicking along on their very high-heeled shoes, always wanting to go faster than she did. Then she added that the city was overrun with dogs, and while trying to avoid a pack of playful German Shepherds she had almost been hit by a *Velo-Solex*. If Paul had responded with any sympathy at all, she might have stopped there. But he didn't, so she went on to say that she also couldn't stand their tiny damp apartment, and what she really disliked most was their bed: with the oversized bottom sheet wrapped around the long tubular pillow they shared, it was impossible to sleep in her normal position. She then said she hated the way he stuck out his chin, the way his lips got, when he spoke French.

Paul sat up and told her that if she really hated it so much she could go home. "When I asked you to try living in Paris for a year, you said yes. Since we got here, you've done nothing but complain and make me feel bad." His voice was trembling.

"If I can't get used to it, I can't," Maxine muttered to herself as she padded down the cool tiled stairway in her bare feet.

She was not all right. It was that simple. After five months of living in France, she still felt as if she had accidentally taken some powerful drug and was so enfeebled that she had no control over what happened to her. She was assailable, exposed. She wanted out.

She stood at the edge of the pool, her hands on her hips. As usual, almost everyone was doing the breast stroke, which was not only silly to look at but dangerous. More than once she had been struck in the chest by a flailing French leg. She slipped into the shallow end, making the two ladies in flowered suits who chatted as they swam move over into one lane.

After two laps Maxine noticed that someone was swimming beside her. A woman in a red and white striped bathing suit was pacing herself with Maxine, her strokes hitting the water, her legs fluttering past, in exactly the same tempo. Maxine smiled to herself under the water. French women didn't usually do the crawl. In another few laps, though, Maxine wished she would go away. She felt she was being copied, or even challenged. She increased her speed. The woman stayed with her. She flung her arms forward, kicked her legs faster, until the water seemed to have thickened and her breath came out in grunts.

The other woman couldn't keep up and stopped at the shallow end, gulping air. Maxine swam on but by the time she tucked her legs at the deep end, her sense of victory had faded, and on her way back down the pool she felt childish and alone. As she approached the woman again, Maxine slowed down, subtly inviting her to continue. The woman understood, lowered her goggles and with a powerful push from the wall, caught up with her again. They swam at a leisurely pace for several laps, then picked up speed, crashing through flip turns and barrelling off again.

At the end of her swim, her shoulders burning, Maxine hoisted herself out of the pool. The other woman continued. The lifeguard, a beefy man in a nylon bikini, folded his arms and grinned at her. She smiled back. They stood together watching the other woman. Bubbles flowed from her heels, leaving a wake like a speedboat. The lifeguard rolled his eyes, then shook his hand as if something were stuck to it.

"Yeah," Maxine said. "Wow."

At swimming pools in Paris men and women shared everything, including the showers. Maxine pressed the button on the wall that started the hot water, turning her body to let the stream flow first over one shoulder, then the other, annoyed at having to take a shower with her bathing suit on. She washed her hair, then her face and arms. The men, at least, could wash their torsos.

The woman in red and white stripes was beside her now. She was tall and her arms looked too slender to pull her through the water as fast as they did. She had a small mark on her face, as if someone had pressed some smooth flat object the size of a dime into her cheek, making a shallow crater. The woman turned to her and said something Maxine didn't catch.

"*Je ne parle pas français,*" she said, hating herself for not having paid attention in class, for not having had the foresight to predict this moment.

"Do you speak English?" the woman asked in an accent so heavy that Maxine almost succumbed to the spasm of nervous giggling welling up inside her.

"Yes, I do. I'm from New York."

"Ah!" The woman's face brightened. "*Fantastique!*"

"Have you been there?"

"No. No English." She smiled sadly and added, "*Je m'appelle Dominique.*"

"*Je m'appelle* Maxine."

"*Maxim?*" it sounded like the woman asked.

"*Oui,*" Maxine answered, because it was close enough and she was not about to quibble with the first French person, other than bus drivers and shopkeepers, who had spoken to her.

"*Tiens,*" Dominique said. "*C'est marrant, Maxim.*"

Maxine didn't know what she was saying, but her expression was friendly, so she smiled.

The man on the other side of Maxine, who had wavy hair and smelled of red wine the way French workers did in the early morning, leaned forward and said something to Dominique. Then Maxine heard the words "American" and "New York" laced with Dominique's accent, making them sound like something juicy and delicious, something that made her mouth water.

She and Dominique walked upstairs to the locker room together and took two adjoining stalls to get dressed. Dominique thanked her although she wasn't sure for what. They emerged simultaneously, but their movements were no longer parallel. They circled each other as they went from shelf to bench to mirror, Dominique applying makeup, Maxine tugging at the knots in her unruly hair. Then she zipped up her boots, rolled up her damp towel. Dominique pulled on a woolen cap and said, "*Bon*! *A demain*?" offering Maxine her hand to shake.

"*A demain*," Maxine said, watching her go up the steps.

She walked back through Luxembourg Gardens, the gravel crunching under her feet. A pair of policemen in long dark capes strolled past, their hands clasped behind their backs, moving with the ease of ice skaters. Their expressions were so serious that she had to laugh. She entered the outdoor market and made her way down Rue Mabillon past piles of bulging purple eggplants "*les aubergines*," she whispered past the butcher shop where she invariably caught sight of something she wished she hadn't. Yesterday it had been a wild boar, hooked by its heels, its dangling snout covered with a plastic bag slowly filling with blood. Today, though, it was only a row of small white rabbits, their lucky paws dangling helplessly. She pushed through the crowd of French shoppers and into the cheese store. One woman picked up a disk of Camembert and firmly pressed her thumb into its center to see if it was ripe. She frowned and put it down again. Maxine felt suddenly tolerant of the French obsession with food. All over the nation, she thought, housewives are squeezing cheeses. She waited her turn, bought six brown eggs that clicked together but did not break in their small waxed paper bag, then went down the street a little further to buy a baguette, *The International Herald Tribune* for herself and *Le Monde* for Paul. He had been a French major in college. She envied him for that.

She opened the apartment door with her oversized key and found Paul putting out the amber glass bowls for coffee, something he usually let her do. He had already shaved and put on a pair of jeans and a white shirt, still unbuttoned. He put his arms around her.

"One more month, okay?" he said. "If I'm not playing somewhere by then we'll go home. I'll call Bill and tell him I have to have my job back early. We'll stay with my parents until we can get our apartment back."

Maxine slipped her arms around his waist. Six years earlier, when they had met at a party in a loft on 19th Street in Manhattan on a densely hot summer night, the first thing Paul had told her was that he wanted to live in Paris and play his saxophone in the jazz clubs. It wasn't just a fantasy, he said. He was really going to do it.

"It's okay," she told him now. "I'm not ready to give up yet."

"It's so stupid," he said, "but I've been wishing for this since sixth grade."

"You're a fine musician," she said.

He held her tightly.

"I'm going to borrow a hundred more dollars on my credit card," she told him over breakfast, dipping her buttered bread into her bowl of coffee and hot milk. "I have to study French."

He reached over to tuck the label back into her blouse.

"I thought you hated French," he said. "I thought you said it was a dead language."

"I changed my mind," she said, tempted, for a moment, to tell him what had happened. But she had a superstitious feeling that if she told Paul, if she even said Dominique's name aloud, Dominique would disappear forever.

"Fine," he said. "Great."

When he cleared the dishes from the table, his supple movements, the muscles in his arms, reminded her of Dominique, and again she thought of telling him. But she didn't.

After that day Maxine set the alarm faithfully every night and slipped out of the apartment every morning, careful not to wake Paul. If he wanted to come along she would be unable to explain why she would rather he didn't. When she walked into the locker room and Dominique was already there, Maxine knew her own face lit up. She was overcome with happiness.

"*Tu es en retard*," Dominique said, closing the door of the locker gently.

"*Oui*," Maxine said, wanting to add that she had overslept, that Paul had come home later than usual and woken her, but not knowing how to say it.

"*Je vais nous faire de la place*," Dominique said, leaving her standing alone, foolishly grinning, while she went off to make space for them in the pool.

Maxine looked around, stricken, as if she were making a spectacle of herself, but everyone else was tucking socks into shoes, hair into bathing caps, paying no attention at all.

That evening Maxine went to the large gray *Alliance Française* building on Boulevard Raspail. The hallways and stand-up cafe were mobbed with fair-haired young students speaking Eastern European languages. Flyers announcing excursions had been slapped up all over the walls. She pictured herself on a bus full of young Poles and Czechs, off to see some national monument. The idea was so depressing she almost turned around and walked out, but the thought of being able to talk to Dominique made her go instead through the door marked *Inscriptions*. A woman behind the counter came forward. Maxine had some difficulty explaining what she wanted. The woman nodded, led her into a large room with tall windows where people were working at carrels, seated her, gave her a test, and told her when she was finished to see one of the examiners. Of the hundred items, she completed only twenty, five of which she wasn't really sure about, and after a brief interview with an exhausted woman wearing very red lipstick, was placed in a level called "false beginners" and told that she could pay for the remainder of the month and begin the following evening.

Over the next weeks, Dominique's swimming grew stronger, and sometimes she swam so fast that Maxine's neck turned red as she stretched her body, grabbing handfuls of water and pulling them under her, curving her back toward the sky. When the pool was crowded, a group of men, also good swimmers and friends of Dominique's, became gallant, found space for them. *Viens-là, les filles.* On those days Maxine and Dominique were pushed together, their shoulders almost touching, their ankles knocking as they careened through their flip turns.

If they completed fifty laps together, Maxine knew that the day would go smoothly. When they got ready to leave she observed Dominique carefully as if to memorize her movements, the sound of her voice, to keep them with her as she travelled through the mist gray streets of Paris to do another temporary typing job at an American company in the sixteenth district. Throughout the day, as she sat on an uncomfortable typist's chair or kneeled by a filing cabinet, odd images of Dominique would flash through her mind: her red-painted toenails, her angular knees, her incredibly narrow midriff silhouetted against the clear blue of the pool's interior. She imagined that Dominique, in an office, would perform the simplest task rolling a piece of paper into a typewriter, for instance with great dignity.

I don't know how to think about this, she thought. I have no model. Then, out of habit, she tried saying it in French. "*Je n'ai pas de modèle*," she whispered.

Her French class was from six to eight in the evening. She sat in the first row and raised her hand whenever the teacher asked a question, but it was only to give the answer to an exercise in the book or to write part of the dictation on the blackboard. The class was too large for conversation.

She often didn't see Paul at all, and was only vaguely aware of him getting into bed beside her in the very early morning. One evening he left her a note, on a page torn from her vocabulary notebook, telling her that he and Michel were going to try a new club, that he had a feeling they were going to get lucky, and if she wasn't too tired, why didn't she meet them there? She pushed it aside and took out her copy of *Le Monde*, spending the next hour looking up words in the dictionary. After struggling through half an article, she turned on the television and watched the news, trying to distinguish words among the sounds and rhythms of the language. She studied the speakers' faces and gestures, imitating the way they rounded their lips.

Soon Maxine began attempting conversations with anyone who would put up with her. The pinched faces of her French co-workers softened when they saw that she wasn't going to force them to speak English, and during breaks they asked her courteous questions about life in New York.

In the month of May there was a change. Her French got better and so did the weather. It stopped drizzling, first of all, and there were extravagant amounts of daylight, as there had been ridiculous quantities of night during the winter. On weekends she and Paul took long walks beside the river, marvelling at the quality of the light. When they got home at eight in the evening, sunlight was still streaming in the window. Paul took out his saxophone and practiced. It wailed and warbled in the fragrant air, and across the narrow street the neighbors leaned out their windows, smiling. They drank a white wine called Sauvignon and their lives seemed charmed, even though Paul still hadn't found a real job that paid money and their time was running out. When

Paul left to make his rounds at the jazz clubs, Maxine went to bed. At ten o'clock it was still not completely dark yet, making her feel like the bad child who had to go to bed early, while Paul, the good child, got to stay out and play.

In the morning Maxine no longer made her way to the pool by moonlight. In fact, it seemed incredible that in February when the clock in the tower at Luxembourg Gardens had struck nine, it had still been night. Now she walked in broad daylight at six in the morning. Now there was daylight to spare. Maxine wondered if it hadn't been the dark that had made her so befuddled.

Her favorite person to talk to turned out to be the locker room attendant at the pool, an immigrant from Mali whose white uniform was spotless and who turned off the hairdryers at exactly eight-thirty whether people were finished using them or not.

"*Ça va?*" she began.

"*Ça va bien, et toi?*" he obliged her.

"*Moi aussi,*" she said. Then she stood in front of him, waiting for more. He had nothing better to do, so he asked her: Did she sleep well last night? Did she have breakfast before or after swimming? Did she plan to continue swimming all summer, or did she only like swimming in winter?

One day Dominique walked in on them.

"*Vous parlez maintenant,*" she said.

The attendant told her that Maxine didn't speak too much but she seemed to understand almost everything. Dominique said it was a miracle. A month earlier Maxine hadn't seemed to understand a word. They looked at her proudly. Maxine smiled from one to the other, as if they were her parents.

Maxine and Dominique went into two stalls to put on their suits, and Dominique asked a series of carefully articulated questions over the partition between them: Why was Maxine in Paris? Was she alone? What did she do?

When she came out, Maxine explained as best she could about Paul, the music, his dream, their money problems, her temporary jobs. Dominique listened with a serious expression. Maxine could hardly believe she wasn't just pretending to understand.

I can help, Dominique said. Him, maybe not. But you, I can help.

Then she took out her bag and wrote her address and telephone number on a slip of paper with graph lines on it. She invited Maxine and Paul to dinner at her house the following evening. Maxine reminded her that Paul went out looking for work in the evening and would have to leave early.

"*Tant mieux*," Dominique said, putting away her pen and slamming her locker door shut.

Maxine followed her down the stairs to the pool, trying to remember what exactly that expression meant. "So much the better," she thought, except that didn't quite make sense.

When they got into the water, Maxine was exalted. She had done it. She had had a real conversation with a French person. And they were going to be friends.

Now we will swim, Dominique said. And tomorrow we will talk about work.

She pulled her goggles over her eyes, then lifted them again.

I am happy to be able to talk to you, she said.

"*Moi aussi,*" Maxine said.

In the very early morning, Paul gently stroked her arm until she realized that he wasn't just appreciating her presence, he wanted to wake her. In her dream, her shoulder had been just about to touch Dominique's, under the water, except that they weren't really human anymore, but sea creatures with glittering scales.

"Guess what," Paul whispered, excitement rippling through his voice.

"What?" she said, laughing.

"Kiss me," he said.

Then she knew that either he had brought her some great gift, which was impossible since they had no money, or something good had happened to him.

"A job?"

"Not just a job," he said. "A contract. Weekends for two months. And then there's another guy who might also be interested in us. All you have to do is be in the right place at the right time. People hear you. Anything could happen."

"That's great, Paul," she said, pulling him closer. "I knew you could do it."

"Me, too," he said. "I knew I could too."

She was almost asleep again when she heard him say, "There's just one catch."

"What's that?" she asked, trying to force her eyes open.

"The first gig is in Amsterdam. We have to play there twice. Once at the beginning and once at the end. I have to take a train in the morning."

"Oh no," Maxine whispered.

"What?" he said. "Are you upset?"

"I got us an invitation to dinner at a French person's house," she told him. "I was going to surprise you. Now I'll have to go there by myself and I won't even be able to talk to her."

She began to cry. Paul was surprised, but tried to act as if she were behaving normally.

"You'll do fine," he told her. "You speak really well now."

"Oh, God," she said. "Get me a tissue."

He got up and came back.

"It's okay," she said, blowing her nose loudly. "I'll be all right. You startled me. It's the middle of the night, you know. Let's go to sleep now, okay?"

"Okay," he said and lay down beside her.

"I'm really happy for you, Paul," she said, still sniffling.

For a while they lay silently side by side. Maxine reassured herself that Dominique was a person who would be undaunted by something so simple as making and serving dinner. She would calmly set each dish before her on a white ceramic plate with a pale blue line around the edge. It would be like a ceremony, like taking communion. Maxine would simply have to sit there and receive it.

"Paul?" Maxine said.

"Yeah?"

"What does *tant mieux* mean?"

It means 'It's just as well,' or 'I'm glad to hear it.'"

"That's what I thought," Maxine said, her heart simultaneously rising and sinking.

"See how much you know?" Paul said.

RUNAWAY

One November morning in my freshman year in college in 1970, I was sitting on the dusty pink sofa in my apartment on Mott and Houston Streets in downtown Manhattan, sipping one of the first cups of coffee I had ever made for myself and contemplating my future, which seemed full of promise, when there was a loud knock on my apartment door.

"Who is it?" I shouted.

"Police," a man answered.

I squinted through the peephole. A man in a felt hat and brown overcoat and a woman about my mother's age were standing on the other side of the door. I opened it.

"Jill Burkhart?"

"Yes?"

"We're sorry to disturb you, Miss," the policeman said. "But we're looking for a runaway. This is the girl's mother." He indicated the teary-eyed woman standing next to him, then handed me a photograph. "This picture was taken two years ago."

The girl in the photograph had a long, sad face and a haircut that her mother must have given her because the bangs were much too short. I had never seen her so I didn't have to lie.

"Her name is Norma. Norma Gabriel. She lived in this building."

I gave back the photograph and shook my head.

"How long have you been living here?" the policeman asked, suddenly exhausted.

"Since September."

He gave me his card, told me to call if I learned anything, and went to knock next door. I waited until they left the building, then ran upstairs to talk to Harry.

Runaway

Harry was a poet and even though he was just a few years older than I was, he knew things. He was paying more attention than I was, he said. In any case, I'd gotten into the habit of asking his opinion about almost everything that happened. Ordinarily, though, I wouldn't have disturbed him in the morning. Harry said he did his best work when he was still close to his dreams.

I tiptoed up the stairs and listened at his door. The doors to our apartments were made of plywood and so thin I thought I would be able to hear his pencil moving. Instead I heard him walking around the kitchen.

"Harry?" I said, knocking softly.

He opened the door, just a little. I squeezed inside and he shut it quickly.

"Are they still out there? You didn't tell, did you?"

"Tell what?" I said. "Gosh, Harry, wasn't it like a movie? The detective, the weeping mother, the photograph?"

Harry pulled his long gray hair into a ponytail with his hands, then looked around the room as if he'd lost something. His apartment was crowded with armchairs and tables. Piles of paper covered with his frantic scribble were everywhere.

"Oh, right," Harry said.

"What?"

I carefully removed a manila folder labeled "Bus Driver poem" from one of the kitchen chairs and sat down. His table, a large wooden spool left behind on the street by the telephone company, rocked on its pedestal.

"I was afraid for a minute that you might have squealed on Norma, and then I remembered that you don't know her."

"Thanks a lot. Who is she?"

"Just a girl. Like you. Except that instead of a stable middle class family she had an alcoholic mother from whom she felt compelled to run away."

Sometimes I hated it when Harry spoke with such grammatical correctness. It seemed unnecessary.

"Norma would come up and bother me all the time," he said. "Like you do. She would play her violin for me. It was very soothing."

Harry was sensitive. The tiny hum of the refrigerator, for instance, drove him crazy. Sometimes he persuaded me to massage his temples.

"You would like her," he told me. "She's childlike but very wise. Small. Your height but much thinner. Painfully thin.

She has a sweet, vulnerable laugh. Laura was wild about her." He frowned. "For a while, anyway." He stood up and stretched. "I have to get back to work."

"Just tell me who Laura was."

"All right." He stood up and opened his apartment door, shooing me into the hallway. "Laura was this thirty-year-old woman who lived with Norma. They were lovers. Then one day she packed up and went back to Illinois. Just like that. Norma was heartbroken." He laughed. "She also had nowhere to live anymore."

"Gross," I said. "Two women."

I couldn't help it. I knew Harry didn't think people should judge each other. He had friends who took drugs and stole cars and he always found reasons to excuse them. But all I could think of was the time in high school when the lights went up after a movie in the auditorium and I saw Joan Parry, the straight-A student, with her white spidery arms around Mary Louise Judson, and how horrible it seemed that they had been fondling each other in the dark.

Harry, of course, was offended.

"What's wrong with it? They made each other very happy for a few months." He narrowed his eyes. "At least Norma had the nerve to fall in love with someone in a whole-hearted way, instead of hanging around with some whiney-butt from Little Neck."

He was referring to me and my friend, Andy.

"You don't have to get mean about it," I said.

Harry was distracted again. "I'm going to try to get in touch with Norma. I'm going to make a few calls."

Andy was waiting for me outside the classroom door. I still had Harry's voice in my head from the first time I told him about Andy.

"Little Neck!" Harry had shrieked. "He grew up in Little Neck? Don't tell me. His father is a policeman and he has a scholarship and he's pre-law."

He was almost right. Andy's father was a fireman. To me it didn't matter. As long as Andy was there, I didn't have to walk into a classroom alone in front of all those well-dressed NYU girls.

"Hey," Andy said when I arrived.

I told him to take off his mirror sunglasses. He did and we went in. Professor Pratt had already started lecturing. He was explaining the significance of the part in *Moby Dick* when Ishmael and Queequeg were having such a good time in bed together. Andy and I took two seats in the back of the room, near the windows.

"Do you see?" Professor Pratt said, his eyebrows quivering. "Everything was a kind of 'double entendre'."

I wrote down the word 'double' and then in parentheses, talk. Andy's laugh hissed through his teeth.

"Great notes," he whispered.

Professor Pratt looked injured. He took it personally when his students weren't listening.

I wrote "Cotton Mather:" and began thinking about Harry's friend Norma. How would it be to have run away from home, to have no apartment, no allowance, no education? The only good thing would be telling people. "I'm a runaway," I imagined myself telling Andy. He would be bowled over. But why would I run away? My parents had given me everything I wanted and the few rules they did have—I couldn't stay out past midnight or on the telephone for more than half an hour at a time—made sense. They did get on my nerves a little. I hated the way my mother plucked at me when I was getting ready to go out. But that wasn't the kind of thing people ran away from home over.

Andy, for some reason, was giggling. I looked up at him, puzzled.

"You were leaning so close to your notebook and concentrating so hard," he whispered. "I thought, 'Wow, this girl takes great notes.' Then I leaned over to have a look."

He started laughing again.

The whole page was covered with exactly the same flower, six petals, a circular center, and two leaves on the stem.

"I was thinking," I said crossly.

He raised his eyebrows and tried to look serious.

"Oh! That's good!"

After class I turned down Andy's offer to have coffee and talk about *Moby Dick*. I wanted to talk to Harry again. I wanted to tell him that I wasn't prejudiced, and if two girls wanted to sleep together that was fine with me. It wasn't really true, but I was afraid Harry would stop being my friend if he figured out how opinionated I was.

Harry worked part-time as a stock boy at the A&P. They had offered him a manager's job but he refused. He needed to rest his mind, he said, and stocking supermarket shelves was perfect. I took a shopping cart and started up one aisle and down the next, looking for him. The thought of Harry making pyramids of canned peas every afternoon for two dollars and seventy-five cents an hour made me feel considerably more respect for him and shame for myself for living off my parents.

Each time I turned a corner I expected to find him, crouched beside a cardboard box, removing the cans one after the other, hand over hand. He would invite me to dinner. "Lobster newburg or beef stroganoff?" he would whisper. It wasn't until I had gone down every aisle that I remembered Monday was his afternoon off.

When I got home I went right upstairs without even stopping at my own apartment and arrived just as he was opening the door for a girl in a Peruvian wool cap with earflaps.

"Norma!" Harry said, pulling her close. Then, before I could slip away, he saw me. "Jill! How convenient of you to get here at the same time."

Norma blushed when Harry introduced us, then took off one of her oversized fur-lined leather gloves and shook my hand, startling me and herself with the gesture. She propped her violin case just inside the door, then took off her coat and shook out her long hair. Harry took her things into the bedroom. He came back and poured us each a Coke, then ushered us into his overstuffed living room. Norma collapsed into an armchair as if she were relieved to finally have a place to sit down, the way I imagined a waitress would. Harry smiled benevolently and maneuvered me into a lumpy chair, keeping the other comfortable one for himself.

Norma was living on 120th Street with a painter named Ralph, she told us, who had just discovered that his lover, Thomas, was a compulsive liar. She and her friend Becky were playing duets in the West Fourth Street subway station and making about sixty dollars a week each.

"What do you do to survive?" Norma turned and asked me.

"Jill doesn't have to worry about survival," Harry told her. "She goes to NYU."

"You have a scholarship?"

"She has parents."

"Does she also talk?" Norma asked him, since I hadn't said a word yet.

"She does," Harry said. "But I don't think you'd like to hear what she has to say about girls of your persuasion."

Norma gave me a sympathetic look.

"That's okay," she said. "I thought lesbians were horrible, too, until I discovered I was one."

I smiled back at her, but her actually having said the word *lesbian* kept me speechless.

"Now," Harry said, getting up and stretching, as if he'd been having a nap, "would be a good time for me to read you ladies my new poem. Let me see if I can find it." He went into the kitchen.

"Do you live here?" Norma asked me.

"In this apartment?" I couldn't believe she thought such a thing.

"No. In this building."

"Yes," I told her.

"Oh," she said, blushing again and pulling her knees up close to her chest. She was as shy as I was.

Harry came back and read us his poem called "I'd like to break your windows, part two." I tried to listen carefully so Norma would know I was smart if not open-minded, but when he finished I could only tell him that I loved the part about "cast iron claps of thunder." Norma made specific comments about almost each line and ended by telling him to stop trying to appear thoughtful and elegant and just say what he meant.

When the lobster newburg had finished baking, Norma insisted that Harry clear the papers off his table and put out dishes so it would seem like we were going to have a real meal, not just stolen frozen food. She found a candle and placemats and a serving platter Harry had forgotten he had.

"How did my mother look, Harry?" Norma asked him when she sat down.

"Not too bad," he told her. "Like she'd been crying."

Norma sighed deeply and put down her fork.

"Poor thing. It's amazing she got herself together to come look for me."

Harry squeezed her arm.

"Don't be upset," he said. "Don't stop eating."

After dinner, I washed the dishes while Harry ate the rest of the ice cream from the container and made grandiose statements about art and music and literature. Norma listened, teasing him. I couldn't get over how she was just a regular person.

"Do we want coffee?" Norma asked, and it seemed for a moment that we were all very grown up.

Harry looked at his watch.

"No coffee. It's eleven. I have to go to sleep."

Norma looked at me and laughed.

"All great poets go to bed at eleven," she said.

"I get my best ideas early," Harry said, abashed. "You know that."

When he brought her coat, Norma reached up and kissed him, tenderly, on the cheek and promised not to disappear again. He seemed grateful.

Norma walked me downstairs to my apartment, then stood next to me while I unlocked it, which took me twice as long as usual since she was watching.

"I'll make coffee if you want," I told her, although I didn't usually drink it so late either.

"That's okay," she said.

"It's no trouble," I said.

She came in and we sat down at opposite ends of the sofa. I forgot to make the coffee and once we were sitting down I felt embarrassed to get up again.

Norma took a strand of her hair and wrapped it around her finger.

"I didn't run away from my mother," she said. "It was my two uncles." She let go of her hair and drooped back on the sofa. "They wouldn't let me practice. They told me the violin was a stupid instrument. They would sit around in their dirty slippers eating egg salad sandwiches and yell at me for playing because they couldn't hear the TV. Once they even hid my violin. I couldn't find it for a week."

"How terrible," I said. But what if she took out her violin right now and offered to play? I had never heard one close up and I had a feeling it was going to be extremely loud. What if I had an impulse to put my hands over my ears?

But Norma was thinking about something else.

"Sometimes I think it would be easier to live somewhere else. But I love this city," she said. "Don't you? But then I know so many people here who work ten or twelve hours a day on their art.

Where else can you find that? Painters and musicians and writers and dancers. All of us working so hard, filling the city with our energy. When I think of that I feel much better," she told me.

I had to admit I had never quite seen the city that way before. Mostly I had seen it as something dangerous and frightening that I had to get through on my way back and forth to class.

Norma sat up straight and looked at me.

"What kind of art do you do?" she asked.

"I'm a student," I told her. "I don't have time to do art."

"But everyone should be doing some kind of art. Don't you think so?" she said.

I couldn't really answer her. "I don't know. I don't have any art to do. I have schoolwork," I said.

"Okay," Norma said, pushing her hair back behind her shoulders. "I understand that. But what do you do to feel really alive? Do you draw? Sing? Dance? Do you go swimming? Are you religious?"

I shook my head, laughing. I wondered if I ever had felt really alive and how I would know the difference. It seemed the strongest feeling I had ever had was fear.

"I feel happy when I'm learning," I told her. "Like when I can understand how history influenced a writer. That makes me really happy."

"Huh," Norma said. She held her face in her hand and thought for a moment. "Maybe you're a scholar."

I felt redeemed.

"Still," Norma said. "Everyone has art in them. You, too, probably, if you could give yourself a minute to find out about it. I could ..." She frowned. "Never mind."

"What?" I said. "You could what?" It seemed really awful that she had an idea that concerned me and then wasn't going to share it.

"I could help you, I was going to say, but then I thought, what business is it of mine, especially after what Harry said upstairs about how you feel about people like me."

Without even thinking about how I was going to say it, I told Norma the truth, which was that I was having the best time I had had since I moved to New York City.

"Huh," she said. There was a pretty long silence. "But is it true that you hate dykes?"

"I've never known any," I told her. "You're the first one I've ever met. And I like you a lot. So I think that means the answer is no."

There were a lot of questions I wanted to ask her, but it didn't seem like the right time. I hoped we could become good enough friends that I could ask her later. I wanted to know how she was so sure she was a lesbian. Wasn't she ever attracted to boys? When she thought about going out on dates, did she imagine herself with girls? Did she wish she were a boy? Did it go with being an artist? Most of all, since I had begun to realize how much I liked her, I wanted to know how I could be sure I wasn't one.

"You know what would be great?" Norma said, interrupting my thoughts.

"What?"

"If you would call that detective and tell him you thought you had seen me. But somewhere else, like Staten Island."

"That would be kind of hard. I've never been there. How would ..."

"You've never been to Staten Island?" she said, amazed. "You've never taken the Ferry and looked back at Manhattan? What time is it?"

"Midnight. Exactly. Why?"

"Never mind. It's too late. Too late for the ferry. Too late for taking the subway ... God, do I hate going up there at night."

"Stay here," I suggested, patting the sofa. "We can ride the ferry tomorrow."

"Could I? You wouldn't mind?"

"No. Except that I don't have an extra blanket."

"That's okay. I'll use my coat."

Then she looked unhappy again.

"You have to go to school tomorrow," she said.

"No, I don't," I told her. "I can miss a class once in a while. It's not like high school."

Her face brightened and I realized I had never cut a class before only because I never had anything better to do. I got out a pair of flannel pajamas and some heavy wool socks for Norma. I had an electric blanket for myself, but I couldn't exactly offer to share my single bed with her. Then she would get the wrong idea.

At least I thought she would. That was another thing I was going to have to ask her about.

Norma undressed in the kitchen and I went into the bedroom. We put sheets on the sofa. She carefully laid her coat on top. It reminded me of high school slumber parties. Except that she never had to go home. She didn't even have one. We could have as many slumber parties as we wanted. I was already imagining the two of us sitting at the kitchen table together in the morning, having coffee and intense conversation.

"Good night," she called when I turned out the light.

I'm not sure how long I had been sleeping, but the next time I opened my eyes Norma was standing over me, shivering, clutching her coat around her frail body.

"Jill," she said. "I'm sorry but it's too cold in here. I can't sleep. I think I'll go sit in a coffee shop or something until it's light out. You really should complain about the heat."

"Wait," I said. "What about our trip to Staten Island?"

She huddled in the coat and stepped from one foot to the other on the cold floor.

"I'll give you my number. We'll go later."

When I imagined her leaving and myself returning to a life that was nothing more than Harry's pontifications and Andy's bad jokes and classrooms full of people who were not my friends, I knew I wasn't going to be able to stand it. I pulled back the covers.

"Get in," I said. "It's warm in here."

"You're not afraid of catching my cooties?" she said.

"I'll take my chances," I told her.

She slipped into the bed and snuggled up to me.

"We're like Ishmael and Queequeg," I told her.

"Who?"

"This sailor and his Indian friend. Never mind. Go to sleep. I'll tell you tomorrow when we're on the ferry."

MADE TO MEASURE

Gran and Mom have the TV on so loud that it's hard not to get distracted but I can't tell them to turn it down because Gran is a little deaf and anyway it's the centennial celebration of the Statue of Liberty, and they're really into it.

Mom wants me to join them on the sofa but I'm not going to. I have things to think about. I have to decide what kind of job I'm going to apply for and where. Then I have to work on imagining myself living in an apartment.

Mom hovers over me during the commercial.

"Take the day off, Helen. It's a national holiday."

"I have to find a job," I tell her.

"Don't make such a big deal out of it," she says.

Sunlight is pouring in the window but it doesn't feel warm because of the air conditioning. Mom keeps telling me to relax. The jobs will be there. I can have my old room back and live with her and Gran for as long as I want. That's like telling someone who's trying to swim across the English Channel to take a break. At this point in my life, momentum is everything.

I go out into the backyard and sit at the picnic table in the sun. A couple of robins are hopping around in the sprinkler on the lawn next door. It's hard to believe that I went away for four whole years and nothing happened to me, and that I'm back again and nothing is happening now, either.

I did go to college. I had a roommate named Carole. I worried that she would tell me at the end of one year that she didn't want to be my roommate the next. She always came back though, until this year, when she went to Ithaca to marry Todd and I came back to Ballston Spa to sit around with my mother and grandmother until I figure out what to do.

I can't decide whether to look in *The Saratogian* or *The New York Times*. How far away do I want to go, exactly?

Made to Measure

It's too hot on the deck and there are bees. Back inside, the crowd on the TV screen seems very orderly, but Mom and Gran and I agree that we're better off safe in our own living room instead of mushed up against any of those people on the screen. Maybe New York City would be too crowded for me.

I have had it with the statue, I tell them, and volunteer to do the laundry. The idea of her size is starting to make me nervous. On TV they keep giving her measurements: length of hand, 16' 5"; index finger, 8'; length of nose, 4' 6". Her waist is 35', one announcer tells us. Her mouth is three feet wide. Her fingernail is 13" by 10". Now they are showing her toes, her enormous feet in their huge sandals. I go down to put the laundry in while Mom and Gran watch the tall ships go by on the screen, one after the other.

When I get to the bottom of the basement steps, I gasp. Someone is standing in the corner. I take a groping step backwards and realize the figure doesn't have a head. It's only my mother's dressmaker's mannequin. Even so, I need a minute to catch my breath, to stop my heart from pounding. I notice that over the years my mother has added to and adjusted the padding, compensating for her changing shape. I begin to feel embarrassed, as if I were staring at her naked body. I stuff the dirty laundry into the machine, handling their underwear with the tips of my fingers, shoving my faded jeans and T-shirts in after them.

I come back up and sit down with them for a minute. My mother lights a cigarette, sucks on it hard, her cheeks going hollow. Gran shows she's unhappy by taking her white embroidered hanky out of her sleeve and fanning the air. I know I should try to persuade my mother to stop smoking, but I just can't. The last time she took it so personally, as if I were asking her to stop breathing.

When Mom and I embraced at the train station, she held her cigarette away from me. "Welcome home!" she said, squeezing me tight with one arm, the other hoisted high behind her. She was soft, like pudding. I pulled away, frightened by the sensation that I was falling.

When we got home Mom went right to the kitchen to make herself a drink. Gran was sitting in her favorite chair, waiting for me to come over and give her a kiss, which I did right away. The next thing I did was go check my room. It hadn't changed. There are two lamps with bulbs shaped like flames. The ends of the four posters on the bed are also flame shaped. Over my bed is the series of photographs of bridges I did in the photography club in college. When I lie down I get to look at the silhouette my second grade teacher did of me. Two black shadows of my profile looking at each other, chopped off at the bust, as if my body were somewhere else.

My room is full of boxes of stuff I brought home from college. I'm not going to unpack them because I'm not staying. I might look through them one afternoon while the two of them are napping, though. Over the years I have become an expert at not waking them up. I monitor my breathing, the scratching of my pen, the heaviness of my footsteps, to prevent vibrations. Carole said I was the quietest roommate in the world, making her the luckiest. For her I even tried not to turn over too often in my sleep, because I noticed that if I turned over, she did, and I didn't want her to wake up feeling tired.

Sometimes she hugged me.

"This is heaven," she said. "This is perfect. I hope Todd and I get along as well as this."

"Drink time," says my mother. I look at my watch. It's only eleven thirty. Gran gives her a worried look.

"It's a holiday," my mother explains. Otherwise she would wait until noon.

Mom didn't always drink so much. Right after Dad died, though, she really got into it. I would come home from school to find her, the curtains drawn, a glass in her hand, watching the soaps. I would go to my room to do my homework. When I came out a few hours later she was watching the news. I could not get her to stir, not even for dinner. Sometimes she would forget to buy food. "Isn't there a can of tuna you could have?" she would ask.

I would sit down beside her and whine. I just didn't know what else to do. I wasn't doing well in math, I told her. I wasn't popular, or pretty. I couldn't make any friends. Slowly she started listening. One day she looked into my eyes and, seeing herself (Gran, Mom and I have exactly the same pair of pale blue eyes) declared she could help. One sure way to improve my appearance would be to have an attractive and varied wardrobe. The most economical way to do that would be to let her sew for me. I could have twice as many outfits as the other girls if they were homemade.

The clothes my mother made for herself were not particularly stylish so I knew mine weren't going to be either, but I agreed. It would be a relief to have her talking to me again.

What I didn't realize was how much time she would need to fuss over me. After dinner she would make herself a nightcap and I would stand on the coffee table while she patted and plucked and smoothed for what seemed like hours. Her mouth full of pins, my mother crouched and measured, adjusted, straightened.

"There," she would say. "How's that?"

At first I would tell her, quietly, patiently, that I didn't think she had gotten it quite right, that she needed to try again. As she became more talented, I allowed myself to become increasingly exasperated. I was also a teenager by then.

"No!" I would scream. It was too long! It was too loose! Was she crazy? Did she expect me to go to school looking like a rag picker? On and on I would go—It was hideous! Where had she gotten this material?—until I was exhausted, and she would begin again: taking in, letting down, taking up, letting out. Her touch became progressively lighter, timorously light, until her fingers fluttered over my knees like butterfly wings, crept across my waist like stealthy daddy longlegs.

"Stop!" I would shout, and she would slowly straighten up and sigh, lighting a cigarette, and wait for my crisis to pass. "All right," I would say after a few minutes, swallowing my tears of indignation. "Go ahead."

Then I got a scholarship and went away to college. When I came back for vacations, I told her that everyone wore jeans and T-shirts and that I didn't need any more clothes. It wasn't really true, but the idea of her sewing for me again made me dizzy, as if getting back up on the coffee table would be like leaning over the edge of the World Trade Center.

Late the next afternoon, after I have exhausted the job possibilities for the day and gotten nowhere, we decide to go for a drive. The sky is filled with heavy, dark, fast-moving clouds.

"Look at the blue," Gran says each time they break. Then she says, "How nice it was of God to make it blue, instead of some other color like red or orange."

"Orange," my mother says. "Ugh."

Gran can't remember what day it is. She asks us over and over, aware that she's asking.

"It's a terrible thing to lose your mind," she tells me, an ironic twinkle in her pale blue eyes. "Don't ever do it."

We get out to look at the mountains. Gran grips my arm and then extends one leg in front of her to study her foot.

"Who told me to wear these big white shoes?" she asks.

"I have an idea," my mother says. "Let's go to the new fabric shop at Pyramid Mall and get something to make you an outfit for your job interviews in September."

"First of all, " I say, "my job interviews are going to be in July. And second of all I don't need any new clothes." She looks stung. "Thank you, anyway," I tell her.

"I'll come in with you," I tell my mother. "But I don't need any clothes."

"I'll wait in the car," Gran says, sensing trouble.

We persuade her to sit on a bench in the shade outside the store. She likes to be where she can watch the people walk by.

The clerk in the fabric shop is like one of the girls I went to high school with, so I feel pretty friendly toward her right away. She has short red hair and the frames of her glasses are also red. I realize, looking at her, how inaccurate it is to use one word to describe both of those colors. She comes toward us, smiling.

"What are you ladies shopping for?" she asks us.

"Something for job interviews," my mother tells her.

She looks puzzled.

"For you?" she asks my mother.

My mother tilts her head back and laughs silently.

"No, no. Not for me. For Helen."

This girl and my mother discuss me as if I were a mannequin. The girl looks at my waist. They both comment on how slim it is. I feel proud and ashamed at the same time. I am probably not a size ten anymore, they tell each other. Probably smaller. The girl goes to get the tape measure. I am not minding any of this for some reason. I am looking forward to having the narrow piece of cloth slipped around my waist by this stranger who lumbers a little. She comes back, her eyes focused on her target, my waist, my hips. She holds me firmly as she measures. She does not hesitate or falter. She kneels on the floor to read the circumference of my hips.

"How much do we subtract for the jeans?" she asks my mother.

"At least an inch. Maybe two," my mother says.

Made to Measure

"Are we making a blouse?" she asks, and before my mother can answer has slipped the tape up under my arms and is measuring my bust. In spite of myself I feel my lungs filling with air.

My mother is standing close to me. Too close. Her hands are bunched up near her chest, her fingers ready. I shoot her a glance that says, "Don't!"

"What kind of a job are you looking for?" the clerk says into my ear as she stretches the tape across my shoulders.

I laugh, a little nervously. I'm not very good at conversation with strangers.

"I don't know," I tell her. "I went to college so I could get a good job. I didn't think about what kind."

"I have a friend who has a real estate office on Main Street in Saratoga," she tells me as she jots down the number of inches. "Do you want me to ask her if she needs someone?"

I know the office she's talking about. There is a mock-up of the center of town in the window.

"Yes, please," I tell her.

"And then if you get the job, you can do something for me," she says.

"Like what?" I ask her.

"I don't know," she says, blushing. Now she's the one who is laughing nervously.

My mother comes back with a bolt of fabric. It is a beautiful pale gray tweed, with flecks of blue in it. It looks more expensive than what she usually offers me.

"This is one hundred percent wool," she says. "So I would have to line it with something."

Right now, with this red-haired girl watching us, it seems not just unpleasant but really embarrassing that my mother is going to make me a skirt.

"Maybe you should learn to sew yourself," the clerk tells me. "Maybe I could teach you."

My mother visibly bristles.

"I've been trying to teach her for years," she says. "She won't learn."

The red-haired girl smiles, as if she knows a secret that my mother and I have missed out on. "I'd have better luck with her, I think," she says.

The clerk measures the fabric and my mother pays for it. Maybe I will learn to sew. The clerk, who hands me a sales slip with her name and phone number on it, is named Carole. This is a good sign, I think.

"Give me a call, Helen," she says, resting her strong hands on the cash register with the same certainty she placed them on my waist earlier. "The real estate office may have an opening for you. I'm gonna ask." We both laugh. Our laughter has the same rhythm now.

"Real estate?" my mother says on the way out.

"You have to start somewhere, Ma," I tell her. "Anyway, think how easy it would be for me to find an apartment. I'd be the first one to see the ads."

On the way home from the fabric store I have a lot to think about but I also have to pay attention to the road because there's repair work going on. We are slowed down by a truck that is leaving a cloud of white dust behind it. This reminds me of a movie that Carole took me to. The old Carole, I mean. My former roommate.

"Have you heard of *The Incredible Shrinking Man*?" I ask my mother.

She shakes her head, exhaling little puffs of pale blue smoke.

"This guy goes through a cloud of radioactive dust," I tell her, "and then mysteriously starts growing smaller. The top scientists and doctors in the world examine him but they decide there's nothing they can do. He just keeps shrinking and shrinking. At first he feels desperate and terrified because he's being chased by the family cat and then by spiders." My mother laughs. "Then, near the end of the movie, he has this revelation that there may be unexplored worlds that are *within* our world, worlds so tiny we can't even see them in a microscope, and he starts feeling optimistic."

"Huh," my mother says.

"So to everyone else," I go on, "it looks like he's just shrinking and pretty soon he's gonna disappear. And his family and friends are sitting around crying. But he knows he's going somewhere really exciting."

"I can see your lips moving," Gran says from the back seat. "But I can't hear a word you're saying."

LILLIAN'S PIANO

Mona is sitting at the kitchen table in our house in Mankato wrapped from head to toe in blankets. She can't get used to the cold. The Hudson Bay blanket that was in the apartment on Jones Street in New York City when I moved there in 1972 is wrapped around her shoulders. The plaid blanket that Jeff brought us from Scotland for our commitment ceremony is wrapped around her thighs. When she said her feet were still cold I went into the blanket box and got out the old blue wool blanket, its satin edging shredded, that I used to take to summer camp, and tucked it around her feet and ankles.

She wants me to tell her stories. She especially likes to hear about what it was like to be a lesbian when I was only eighteen since the idea came to her much later than that. She sips her cocoa.

"Tell me about Lillian," she says.

Outside, sleet hits the window like someone is throwing a handful of rice at it.

Twenty years ago, when I was in college in New York, I had a friend named Dawn, a student at the Manhattan School of Music who worked as a housekeeper for a concert violinist. She did the shopping, cooking, and cleaning, and served the woman all of her meals in bed (the worst part of it, she told me). In return she received room and board in the Sutton Place apartment and permission to invite her friends to the violinist's parties. It was at one of these parties that I met Lillian. I was sitting at the dining room table, under the crystal chandelier, trying to embark on a conversation with an earnest boy in a tweed jacket, when a very tall woman surrounded by men, like a Duchess and her entourage, appeared in the doorway. She removed her red crocheted hat, shook out her long dark hair, stepped out of her shoes and onto the dance floor. The men followed her.

On the dance floor she stamped and twirled, then stood swaying to the music, her arms raised high above her head, her hair rippling down her back, as if she were some magnificent underwater plant, buffeted by the currents. A hush spread through the room, starting with the people closest to her and moving in concentric circles toward the rest of us.

"That's Lillian," the boy told me, grabbing another slice of smoked salmon. "She's given up piano."

When the music stopped, Lillian looked lost. One of the men led her to the punch bowl. For a moment I had the impression that they hadn't just come to the party with her, but were her guardians. Lillian took the glass of punch she was handed, tossed back her hair again, and sat on the sofa, resting her stockinged feet on the marble-topped coffee table. The men wandered off into the crowd. For a few minutes I lost sight of her. When I looked up again she was looking right at me.

I continued asking questions of the boy in tweed when had he first realized he wanted to be a musician? How many hours did he practice a day? but I was distracted. Lillian was staring. I felt that at any moment I would stand up and walk across the room, zombie-like, to where she was sitting. "Yes," I would whisper, without even hearing the question.

But when the music started again, it was Lillian who stood up. Please, I wanted to say to the boy, stop talking and give me a chance to concentrate. Lillian called the men.

"Come with me," she told them, in a softer voice than I would have expected. "I want to show you something."

They strode across the room and stood over me, tremendously tall.

"Look at her," Lillian said. "Isn't she beautiful?"

For a moment even I thought it might be true, if she said so. The men reached down for my arms, pulling me up and out onto the dance floor. We were all supposedly dancing together. Except that I was dancing with Lillian in a circle of men. I don't remember but I think that hours passed, I think the whole party went by, and we just kept on dancing. Once my friend, Dawn, tried to get my attention, but I pretended not to see her. Then the music suddenly stopped and the party was over.

"Bodies are beautiful," Lillian whispered to me as she walked toward the bedroom to get her coat. "They should touch."

I followed her.

The taxi rattled and bumped down Second Avenue, squealed around a corner and roared East, then shuddered to a halt on Tenth Street between Avenues C and D. The two men dismounted from the jumpseats, walked us up three flights of stairs, then waited politely while Lillian unlocked the door.

"Good night," Lillian said to them when we were inside, kissing first one of them, then the other, full on the mouth. "Come see me."

She closed the door.

"Now," she said, turning to me. "Let's find out who you are."

With slow deliberateness she began unbuttoning, first my coat, then my blouse, gradually peeling them off until there was a small pile of my clothing, then her own, near the door. Enthralled, I let her continue, even though I was sure I could hear someone breathing.

One by one, cats wandered lazily out of the kitchen, rubbing up against her calves, nuzzling my ankles. They seemed to awaken her need for privacy. She scooped up our clothing.

"Let's go to my room," she said, leading me down a narrow hallway. We lay down together on the king-sized foam mattress that was her bed. She lit a candle and looked at my face.

"Are you surprised by this?" she asked me. "Are you afraid?"

Her shadow flickered on the wall behind her. I managed to shake my head no.

Mona leans forward, handing me her cup to refill with cocoa.

"But you were terrified, right?" she says.

"Absolutely. I'd never done it before."

"What did she do first?"

"Don't you remember?"

She grins.

"Sort of. But I want you to tell it to me again."

Lillian lay down beside me on the bed and began stroking my body, slowly, in wider and wider concentric circles, nothing but that, nothing you could really call sexual, for what seemed like hours, until I finally spoke.

"Please," I said.

"Please what?"

"Touch me," I whispered.

"I am touching you," she said, gently mocking.

"Touch me here," I said, taking her hand and placing it between my thighs.

"Oh," she said. "There."

When we came out of the bedroom the next morning, Lillian's younger sister, Esther, was sitting at the kitchen table, stringing beads. The living room was filled with the dark presence of the grand piano Lillian had inherited from her music teacher and then never touched. Esther rearranged her long straight hair and gave us a sidelong glance that to me indicated she knew exactly what we had been doing and did not approve. I felt shy, exposed, a little embarrassed but Lillian, I soon learned, didn't care what people thought.

Lillian worked as a legal secretary. She could type a hundred words a minute. She sat up very straight, her eyes fixed on the page, her long, slender hands fluttering across the keyboard, barely seeming to touch the keys. She took no pride in her work and came home from her job crushed and exhausted. Sometimes if her sister was not going to be there she asked me to come over and study at her kitchen table, so that she wouldn't have to come home to an empty apartment. It wasn't my favorite place to work. The cats walked all over my books and papers, harassing me even after I had fed them. When Lillian arrived, she would lean over and kiss me, then fill the clawfooted bathtub in the kitchen with steamy water and bubbles and climb into it to soak. I would get in with her, and let her lean back on me.

"Tell me what you love," she asked me. "Tell me who and what you love. Don't be afraid to tell the truth."

"I love you," I told her.

She smiled sadly.

"Besides me," she said.

I told her that I loved my best friend, Marlene, because she had courage and tremendous energy, and that I loved irises for their shape and color, and that I loved the sound of the wind in the tops of pine trees.

"More," she said.

I told her that I loved to gallop through the woods on a horse, to meet a person who understood what I was talking about, to be awakened by the smell of the sea.

"I used to love piano," she said. "I loved it more than anything."

"Why did you stop?" I asked her.

"I don't know. My teacher died. Maybe it's that. Maybe it's something else. I don't know."

Groups of people drifted into and out of Lillian's apartment like the tides. I began to get to know some of the ones who came back often. Tom, a small, wiry man who was one of the group who had escorted Lillian to the party, announced one night that he had lost his job with a credit card company and decided to use his card to take us out to dinner every night until the company invalidated it. Then, he said, he would move to California. On the first night we went to Molfeta's. Lillian loved Greek appetizers. When the platter arrived she leaned close to the table, hungrily picking out oily black olives and feta cheese and grape leaves, licking her fingers after each bite, brushing away her hair with the back of her hand. Tom and I sat across from her, watching her eat, hardly looking away or taking anything for ourselves, not wanting to miss a single moment.

"Look at her," he whispered to me.

He didn't have to. I couldn't stop. Tom had once been Lillian's lover too, and sometimes I suspected he still was, but I didn't mind having him around because I could tell that he loved her almost as much as I did, if not in exactly the same way.

Lillian sucked the juice from her fingers and watched us watching her.

"Oh, you two," she said. "If I could just add the two of you together."

She needed someone bigger than either of us, she said. She needed someone who deserved to be yielded to, someone big enough for her to lose herself in. There was no use in our trying to talk her out of this idea. She knew what she wanted.

Once she had mentioned this notion of size, it became a preoccupation of mine. I began to live in dread of the tall bearded man in a plaid flannel shirt I imagined was going to stride into her life, taking her away from me. I grew nervous when the super, a large burly Ukrainian who wore his tools on a wide leather belt, came to replace the washers in the kitchen. Lillian said his accent would drive her crazy, although she liked the smell of his cigars. I began to persuade her to stay home from parties. Even though I knew how much she loved, even needed, to dance, I was so afraid that it was there, on the dance floor, that she would meet him. When we did go, the tall men stood out like beacons. "What do you think of that one?" I would ask, in the most nonchalant voice I could manage. "Too effeminate," she would sigh.

Tom's luck with his credit card expired and he moved to San Francisco to start a new life. He and Lillian said a tearful goodbye and then she hardly seemed to miss him. She began to cook. She took pleasure in selecting, washing, chopping the food. She gave me things to touch—the inside of an avocado from which she had just removed the pit, a lichee nut. "Feel this," she would say. Sometimes, in the middle of the night, I would feel one of her hands moving across my back, as if it were remembering a keyboard. Sometimes I would wake up to the sound of the tiny thrust and pull of her crochet needle, and find her sitting up beside me in the dark, crocheting another hat, another scarf.

"What is it?" I would ask her. "What's wrong?"

"I can't sleep," she told me. "My hands won't let me sleep."

One evening we were sitting at the kitchen table, drinking white wine and waiting for the potted chicken to cook, when Esther came home with a small friendly looking young woman named Becky. She had known Lillian before, when she still played. Becky stopped to admire the piano on her way in.

"She doesn't play anymore," Esther told her.

"Lillian?" Becky said, a frown on her long pale face. "How can you resist? How can you have this beautiful instrument and not touch it?"

For a while, Lillian didn't answer. Then she walked out and placed her hand on the dark wood. She ran one finger across it, gathering dust.

"I don't know," she said. "I don't know what happened. It's been out of tune for so long I'm afraid I've ruined it."

"Oh, Lillian," Becky said, her hands on her hips in disgust. "Get it tuned. If you don't want it, I'm sure I could find someone who does."

"All right," Lillian said. "Could we talk about something else?"

Becky told her about her classes at Julliard. Her teachers said she was going to be a concert cellist.

"I'll come back," Becky said, "when the piano is ready. We'll play duets. You'll see how easy it will be."

Lillian stood up very straight and pushed back her hair, more serious, more alert, than I had ever seen her before.

"She's right," Lillian said. "She knows what she's talking about."

The next evening she came home from work, took out a soft cloth, and carefully dusted the piano. She opened the cover, sat on the bench, and placed her hands on the keyboard. Then she got up again and began leafing through the Yellow Pages.

"I have to get it tuned first," she said. "I can't touch it until it's tuned. Mrs. Tarnowsky would kill me." Her eyes filled with tears as she spoke.

By the following evening she was playing. I arrived later than usual and heard her from down the hall. Esther let me in, her finger to her lips. I sat in the kitchen and listened. It seemed to me that she played as well as anyone I had ever heard, but who was I to judge? She played some children's music written by Bartok, then harder pieces by Chopin, Mozart, Beethoven. The luster of her dark hair matched the gleam of the wood. The smooth movements of her hands and body fit into the sounds she was producing. Her expression reminded me of a canoe gliding across still water. The world is perfect for her right now, I thought. Then, in the middle of a sonata she suddenly stopped and began to cry.

She called me.

"Come here," she said. "I'm afraid."

I sat down on the bench beside her and put my arms around her. She buried her face in my neck. I inhaled the sweet smell of her hair and asked her, "Afraid of what?"

"I don't know," she said. "I can't do this alone."

Another week passed. Becky called and arranged for the musical evening to take place. I helped Lillian decide what to wear, then took a bath with her, soaping her neck, her knees, her ankles.

"Do you still love me?" she asked. "Will you always love me?"

"Of course I do," I told her. "Of course I will."

When we were out of the tub and dressed and sitting in the kitchen, Becky arrived. She leaned down to kiss Lillian's cheek, then shook my hand. I knew from her firm, warm handshake that she would bear me no malice, but that she would ask Lillian to stop seeing me and that Lillian would say yes.

Esther sat on the bench beside her sister and turned the pages as she played. Becky held the cello tight between her knees, her blond head tilted thoughtfully. Lillian rocked as she stroked the keyboard. I went back into the kitchen and shooed the cats off my neglected research paper.

Mona sighs. She's starting to feel a little warmer. But there's something wrong with the ending of my story, she tells me. I couldn't have just gone back to my school work. What really happened?

I go to the stove to put on some more hot water.

"That was it," I tell her. "Lillian went back to playing piano. Eventually she stopped calling me."

"So you were like her nurse. Did she become a concert pianist?"

"She moved to New Jersey. She got married and had a kid."

I go out to the living room, sit down on the sofa and flick on the TV with the remote key. Queen Latifa is on MTV, saying she's had it up to here. I wish we could talk about something else now. The part of the story that I never tell is about how Lillian always told me that she wasn't really interested in women, that she was going to get married and have kids some day, that her relationship with me had nothing to do with who she really was but could only happen because the music had gone out of her life. This part of the story was still too embarrassing to admit. It was as if being with me was like having the flu.

Mona hauls herself and her blankets out of the kitchen and snuggles up next to me on the sofa.

"I'm glad she went back to her piano," she says. "Otherwise I might never have met you."

"Me, too," I tell her.

The wind rattles the window frames, tossing another handful of sleet against the glass.